HUB CITY MENACE 2

AVENGE THY BRETHREN

J. WHITE

LOCK DOWN PUBLICATIONS AND CA$H PRESENTS

Lock Down Publications

P.O. Box 944

Stockbridge, GA 30281

www.lockdownpublications.com

Like our page on Facebook: Lock Down Publications

www.facebook.com/lockdownpublications.ldp

STAY CONNECTED WITH US!

Text **LOCKDOWN** to 22828 to stay up-to-date with new releases, sneak peaks, contests and more…

Like our page on Facebook:
Lock Down Publications

Join Lock Down Publications/The New Era Reading Group

Visit our website:
www.lockdownpublications.com

Follow us on Instagram:
Lock Down Publications

Email Us: We want to hear from you!

PART I

"AS DREAMS UNFOLD..."

CHAPTER 1
ANYTHING FOR REVENGE

"How far am I willing to go for revenge? Kid, in order to repay Big D for the heinous acts he committed, I will personally break my oath and every law I enforce daily to condemn his soul to the pits of hell, as well as anyone within his bloodline," Detective Sullivan spoke to Terry and meant every word.

"Sounds to me like this BIG D character has cut you deep. Almost as deep as his hoe ass nephew has cut me. What did he do, other than the obvious?" Terry questioned. He knew of BIG D, but didn't know him.

"I'd rather not speak of that evil and get too worked up. What I would like to know is what other information you can give me on this Marcus Cook guy, and for you to tell me in detail what exactly your plans are for your retribution," Sully probed.

Terry wasn't big on putting people in his business, especially strangers and law enforcement, but he needed Detective Sullivan in his corner. He needed that veil of protection for the shit he was about to do. By the time Terry finished informing Detective Sullivan on his wicked intentions the man was completely flabbergasted.

"My God, BIG D was as evil as they come. But you! You are downright sinister! You know what though, this is exactly what we need. I now see the only way to defeat evil is with greater evil. I will handle Marcus, and we will let that blow sink in. As soon as the dust settles, you may begin to wreak havoc and exact your wrath. You have my word you will be protected and no legal troubles will come your way, so long as this plan stays between us. I'm going to tell you now though, anyone related or in deep with BIG D is to be considered dangerous, so be careful," Sullivan said before extending his arm for a handshake.

As they shook in agreement, Detective Sullivan said, "By the way, what's your name, kid?"

"In this partnership between me and you, names aren't important, actions are. But for the sake of communication, if need be, you can call me T.J."

"Well, Mr. T.J., here's my card. Call if you ever need me. Although, it would be best if we actually never spoke again, considering what the future holds."

———

"OKAY BABY, you be careful now. Behave yourself and remember to call me. Don't be up there at that school actin' a fool. Your ass ain't too old or too big to be beat!" Mecia said to her youngest son Marcus, as they said their goodbyes.

Marcus was finally leaving the nest and on the way to college. She was saddened by his departure, but also proud as a parent should be.

"Don't go off and forget your ole' momma now," she said seriously.

"C'mon, Ma, you know better than that. If it weren't for you, I wouldn't even be here, so I could never forget you. I love you. I'll call later and I'll be by to visit at the end of the week," Marcus said sincerely, before leaving his childhood home and heading into adulthood.

Marcus was a good kid who was destined for great things. He had his whole life in front of him. But as we all know, sometimes life is short. From the day we enter this world and take our first breath, our days are numbered and no one but God really knows when their time will be up.

————

PURE JOY AND EXCITEMENT FILLED MARCUS' heart, as he backed out his mother's driveway. As he drove the path to his destination, he couldn't stop smiling ear to ear. In no time, he was within minutes of the enormous campus. Since Marcus grew up in the city, he'd seen the Texas Tech University campus at least a million times, but this time seeing the school was completely different. He felt in his bones he was about to be a part of something great, something special!

Drawing closer to his new home, Marcus decided to celebrate somewhat and listen to one more song before his arrival. He turned up the volume as high as it would go, catching the tail end of one of his favorite songs, "I'm Not Racist" by Joyner Lucas.

"I'm not racist, but I cry a lot/You don't know what it's like to be in a frying pot/You don't know what it's like to mind your business and get stopped by the cops and not know if you 'bout to die or not/You worry 'bout your life, so you take mine/I love you but I fuckin' hate you at the same time/I wish we could trade shoes or we could change lives/So we could understand each other more but that'll take time/I'm not racist/It's like we livin' in the same buildin', but splittin' the both sides/I'm not racist/But there's two sides to every story and now you know mine/Can't erase the scars with a bandage/I'm hopin' maybe we 'can come to an understandin'/Agree to disagree and we can have an understandin'/I'm not racist..."

As the socially conscious song concluded and the beat began to fade from the bass boosted speakers, Marcus' eyes graced the rear-view mirror, after hearing a sound most men in this day and age have grown to fear, police sirens!

The next events to follow only heightened the irony of the oh-so-real rap lyrics Marcus was in tune with just seconds prior.

"Shit!" Marcus cursed out loud as he wisely pulled over into a surprisingly bare IHOP parking lot on the corner of N. University and 19th Street.

Immediately, beads of sweat began to trickle down his forehead when his Maserati came to a complete stop and the Black Crown Victoria swiftly pulled in right behind him, with the cherry on the roof still flashing.

Marcus was a nervous wreck, still sitting in the driver's seat motionless, with both hands on the wheel. Under Jax's careful watch all his life, Marcus had never even come close to breaking the law. He wasn't speeding. He had a license, insurance and any other requirements needed to operate the vehicle, so he was puzzled as to what could be the reason for the stop.

True enough, Marcus was young and had a lot to learn, but he was not totally naïve to the wicked ways of the world. He was well aware of the raging epidemic in America, which was police or any other authority figures killing unarmed black males at an alarming rate, for no reason in most cases. Armed with this public knowledge, Marcus didn't dare make any sudden moves as he watched the pale officer in dark sunglasses approach the driver's side window, hand planted firmly on the butt of his firearm.

The names Tamir Rice, Mike Brown, Oscar Grant and many more flashed through Marcus' mind. He said a silent prayer in hopes that he would not suffer the same fate as they did, all at the hands of those who swore to protect citizens of this country, no matter their shape, size or color.

"Hello, Officer, what seems to be the problem?" Marcus asked nervously.

The man peered down at Marcus with a smirk and said, "Actually, it's Detective... Detective Sullivan," with pride.

"My apologies, Detective. So, how may I help you? Have I done something wrong?" Marcus questioned, still stiff as a board.

"That's exactly what I'm here to find out, kid. Now tell me, is your name Marcus Cook?" Sullivan asked, already knowing the answer based on the information given by Terry.

"Yes, sir, I am Marcus Cook. May I ask what this is all about, Detective?" Marcus spoke cautiously.

"Mr. Cook, are you aware that you have been wanted for questioning in connection to a double homicide for approximately two weeks now?" Sullivan let the lie roll off his tongue fluidly.

Marcus' heart rate quickened, and his breaths shortened in awe of the detective's fictitious statement.

"Sir, there has to be some kind of mistake. I–I'm sure of it. There's no way it could be me you're looking for."

"Well, I'm sure if that's true, we can clear this issue up with no problem and I'll send you on your way. All I need is to run your info through my computer system, and we'll know the truth within a matter of minutes. May I see your license and registration, please?" Sullivan asked, as his eyes quickly scanned his surroundings once more. He was about to do the unthinkable.

"Yes, sir, no problem," Marcus said respectfully. He was scared as fuck! "I'm going to lift up just a bit and retrieve my wallet from my back pocket now." Marcus did as he said slowly and watched the Detective's grip tighten on the deadly weapon, while the man watched him like a hawk. In a snail-like fashion, Marcus retrieved his license and handed it over to the detective through the window.

As if unpleased, Sullivan said, "Registration please," with slight irritation. Marcus felt like something was extremely off and indeed it was. But he followed the orders given to him.

Sullivan stood a mere foot-and-a-half away from the Maserati door, waiting with grave anticipation for the moment only seconds away. A sliver of reprisal that took almost sixteen years to gain. Sending BIG D away to a cushy federal penitentiary all those years ago did nothing for the misery and emptiness of his life without Nancy. In order to remotely feel whole again, Sully wanted an eye-for-an-eye.

In the same slow pace, Marcus reached over and moved to open the glovebox. Pulling the lever, Marcus instantly noticed a difference in the weight of the compartment door but ignored it as the glovebox swung open. He stuck his right hand in blindly and felt the cold steel press against his finger-tips. Unknowingly, he'd just placed his fingerprints on the exact automatic weapon that claimed the lives of D. Lee and Greedy B.

Before he had the chance to make sense of the set-up occurring in real time, Detective Sullivan withdrew his weapon and opened fire at close range, emptying the clip on his unsuspecting victim in broad daylight.

All seventeen shots fired hit the intended target and pushed Marcus' soul away from the earth. As Sullivan's murderous rage subsided, he spoke, "Sorry, kid, you were just a means to a very necessary end."

He truly wasn't the least bit remorseful for his recent actions. In fact, he felt better already having finally avenged the death of his late wife, whose life was snuffed away at the hands of Marcus' uncle BIG D years ago.

After savoring the moment for as long as possible, Sully picked up his walkie and called in the situation at hand, using whatever code law enforcement now uses for cold blooded murder by cop.

Sullivan's only regret in the matter was now once more Texas Tech's football team was hopeless, all at his selfish hand. But he deemed it a small price to pay. Over the years he'd always told himself he'd do anything for revenge... Anything!

CHAPTER 2

A MOTHER'S INTUITION

"Hey, son, you busy?" Mecia asked Jax when he answered his cell. She was lonely at home, pushing through a boring Monday and for some odd reason she was having the weirdest feeling about the wellbeing of her children...

"Uh, kind of... I'm in the studio to do a collab with 3BG and the City Girls, so it's a lil hectic at the moment, but you know you my favorite lady so I can always make time for you. What's up?" Jax replied smoothly.

"Oh, nothing much. You know I'm just a lonely old bear when you kids aren't here. Marcus left this morning and ever since then, I've been having this strange feeling... You think he's okay?"

"C'mon, Ma, don't be paranoid. I'm sure that boy is fine. I mean, he's right down the street. It's not like he's somewhere in a whole other city. I'ma keep my eyes on him of course, but we have to let him live."

"I guess you're right, son. I just miss my baby already," Mecia admitted. "I should have went with him to help him unpack and settle in. You know Marcus is a mess. Po chile," she laughed.

"Haha, yeah, that's true! But sooner or later, he's gonna have to learn to be a man and not a momma's boy," Jax added more seriously.

"Also true," Mecia agreed. "Anyway, that church event I had going on today was rescheduled until tomorrow, but I'm not feeling so hot today. So, do you think you could still go pick up my prescription for me, dear?"

"Yes, Ma'am. As soon as we finish up here, I'll get right on it and I'll be by later this evening," Jax promised. He had completely forgotten about the favor Mecia asked of him the last time he saw her.

"Thank you so much, son."

"It's nothing, Ma."

"Well, before I let you go, have you heard from Ke' today?" Mecia asked. She wanted to make sure all her children were good. She just couldn't shake the feeling that something was wrong with someone.

"Yeah. Ke' texted me before she went to class asking about the next video shoot. She's good. She'll be by to see you later too."

"Okay then, son. I guess Momma's going to go take a nap. I love you and will see you later. Bye, sweetie," Mecia said sweetly.

"Alright, Ma. I love you too!" Jax said and ended the call.

Terry entered the room as Jax's call ended.

"Wassup, boss man, you good?" Terry asked Jax with clear sarcasm.

"What I keep tellin' y'all bout that boss shit?" Jax chastised him.

"Chill," Terry threw his hands up, "I'm just fuckin' with

ya', Jax. But, nah for real, you good?" he asked, hoping the answer was no.

"Yeah, I'm straight, that was just my moms checkin' in."

Terry fought to hide the disappointment in his eyes. He thought for sure that was the call Jax would be receiving delivering the tragic news of Marcus' death.

"Aye, T.J., I know you're supposed to be preparing for your solo studio session here in the next few hours, but I'm swamped in work right now with 3BG and the City Girls. Do you think you could do me a huge favor, man?" Jax asked while simultaneously listening to one of the verses the ladies were spitting on the opposite side of the Plexiglass.

"Sure thing, my nigga. Shit, what you need me to do?"

"Could you run over to Les' Pharmacy over on East Avenue A and pick up my T-Lady's script for me? I know that ain't your job or mom, but I can't leave right now. I have to make sure we get this track done before the deadline, and if I burn off and leave all these divas with Stephen, ain't no tellin' what might happen, knowing these feisty ass women and their 'my shit don't stink' attitudes."

"Hahaha," Terry busted out laughing. "I feel you on that, man. Yeah, I can handle that for you though. Want me to go right now?" he asked.

"Yeah, man, just so we don't have to worry about it later. The script's under Mecia Cook. You can take my whip," Jax said, tossing over the key to his new Bugatti. "Aye, but if you fuck my shit up, you gone have to buy me a new one when your first advance clears," Jax joked but was still quite serious.

"No worries, I'll treat her good and be back in no time," Terry said over his shoulder as he made his exit.

———

TERRY DROVE the super sporty vehicle like he was fleeing from a deranged psychopath, pushing the limits on the digital speedometer after each turn. Everyone in the city knew the Nipsey Blue Bugatti Chiron to be Jax's car, so other motorists on the road that day cursed his name as the car flew past them recklessly. Due to the heavy window tint installed by Hot Boi, no one could actually see the driver was in fact, not Jax.

As Terry pulled up to the pharmacy, he took note of a nice, souped-up truck in the otherwise lonely parking lot. In his opinion, the truck seemed so out of place, assuming the pharmacy was most likely run by uppity white folk who surely owned a Benz or a Jaguar, not the customized monster he parked next to. Terry had agreed so quickly to do this favor for Jax not only to stay in his good graces, but so he could personally make progress on his nefarious ulterior motives.

It wasn't long before this particular day when he learned Mecia took medication for some heart condition he wasn't fully aware of, when he snooped through her medicine cabinet in the bathroom of her home, at the dinner following Greedy and D. Lee's funeral.

He found it quite strange that this wonderful opportunity fell into his lap so easily.

Ding-Ding!

The overhead doorbell rang out as Terry entered the front of the small building.

The bell gathered the attention of the female associate behind the counter, and she called out, "I'll be with you in just one second," in an even tone. She was facing the opposite direction, bent over, placing a few loose items on a low shelf.

"Damn, she got that ass!" Terry said to himself just over a whisper. From where he was standing at the counter, he had a full view of the woman's well-sculpted derriere. The sight instantly sent a wave of hot-blooded thought to his sexually famished brain.

Every single sexual idea he concocted rushed from his mind, the second the lady rose up and turned to face him. Suddenly, it was as if he was staring in a mirror. The lady on the other side of the counter resembled him in a scary, identical twin-like fashion, minus his peach fuzz and tapered haircut.

However, she didn't seem to notice any of the stunning similarities Terry had.

"Welcome to Les' Pharmacy, how can I help you, sir?"

Still stuck on her likeness to him, Terry completely ignored her question.

"Excuse me, sir, how can I help you?" she reiterated.

Snapping out of his trance-like state, Terry was finally able to lift his tongue. "Yes, uh, sorry. I'm here to pick up a uh, a prescription for a friend," Terry said to the lady, never breaking eye contact with her. "Um, the name is Cook. Mecia Cook," he followed up with.

"Oh, okay. How's Miss Cook doing now anyway?" the lady asked.

"Uh, she's good," Terry replied.

"Well, you usually don't pick up Miss Cook's scripts, so where is Jax?"

Just the mention of Jax's name gave Terry a pause, in search of a reply. Then once again, he was caught off guard by their identical features as he studied her face, allowing his tongue to go slack.

"Um, is everything okay, sir?" the lady asked. The vibe between the two was growing quite awkward.

Terry shook back and said, "I'm sorry. I don't mean to be weird, it's just looking at you, I can't help but feel I know you. Have we ever met before?" The puzzling look on his face was clear. He was serious.

"I doubt it. I don't get out much and I don't even live here in Lubbock anymore, I just work here," the lady informed.

"But you have before?" Terry asked.

"Before what?" the lady raised her arched brows, perplexed.

"Lived in Lubbock," Terry shot back.

"Oh, yeah... sure, a long time ago."

Terry couldn't shake the feeling that settled in the pit of his stomach. Growing up with Terrance, his older brother, was a bit difficult because of the gap in their ages, but he loved him to death. They both were abandoned by their mother when they were young and left to live with their aging grandmother in the heart of the projects.

Back then, Terry was too young and too green to really grasp everything. But he did retain a few early childhood memories that involved another sibling. A twin sibling in fact. And according to Terrance, if Terry remembered correctly, his twin was a girl named Tory.

"Can I ask you what your name is?" Terry asked. He'd looked beforehand at the lady's shoulder area, just above the curve of her breast, but no telling name tag was present. His curiosity had gotten the best of him.

"My name is Tory, yours is?"

"Terry."

When Terry spoke his name aloud, a light of recognition

sparked behind the membrane of Tory's gray pigmented irises. Suddenly, Tory began to notice everything Terry had. It was clear now how much the man standing in front of her resembled her in every way, minus the fact that he was clearly a male, lacked her full figure and fiery red hair.

Now Tory automatically began to unconsciously recall distant memories of her growing up with her twin sibling. Sometimes when her late mother Sharon was free from the death grip of Les and sober enough to engage in meaningful conversation, she would tell her beautiful stories about her long-lost siblings. Especially stories that tended to highlight Terry.

"Let me see your hand," Tory said, extending her hand toward his resting on the glass countertop.

Terry looked at her suspiciously, but inched his hands closer to her so she could see them. Tory remembered how Sharon told her one day that she and her twin brother shared the most unique birthmark. A birthmark, that when matched parallel to each other created the unmistakable image of a heart.

As Tory placed an awkward angled hand next to Terry's from the opposite side of the counter, both of them held their breath, knowing what they were bound to see. An evident symmetrical heart symbol formed before their eyes when her left and his right hand made the slightest contact.

Although they knew what to expect when pairing hands, the whole ordeal still seemed quite surreal. The shock of the inevitable truth made them both withdraw their hands from each other and create space between them. It was clear that neither of them awoke that morning expecting to meet one another. Especially not in the way they had.

As fate would have it, for both Terry and Tory, this

reunion couldn't have come at a better time. Tory was at a point in her life where she really needed somebody, anybody to help her escape the hell she'd been forced to live in. For Terry, he needed a familiar face in his life to help fill the void of emptiness. He wanted someone in his corner to help him capture the happiness that eluded him all his life. But even more so, he needed someone with the pharmaceutical knowledge he was sure Tory possessed.

The two carbon copies stared at each other in awe, it seemed now that they were aware of each other's identities, their brains were now synched in telepathic-like communication. In that very moment, they both knew they would be extremely beneficial to each other in some way or another. Nothing needed to be said.

———

No MATTER how hard she tried, Mecia just could not get comfortable enough to fall asleep. She tossed and turned restlessly for over an hour before she gave up and got out of bed.

In efforts to boost her diminished energy, she made it to the island in her kitchen and proceeded to make a steaming pot of coffee. As small dribbles fell down into the awaiting pot, Mecia zoned out, losing herself in deep thoughts. Since her home was mostly empty nowadays, she had a lot of alone time to sit back and reflect on her life. She was a proud single mother to four incredibly accomplished children and that thought alone warmed her heart.

Her health was better than it had been in past years. The spiritual connection she shared with God was unbreakable and all of her family was alive and well. In all, Mecia couldn't really ask for more.

To the naked eye of someone on the outside looking in, it would seem like Mecia had it all, but there was one thing she truly longed for... love.

Not like the love she received from her children or extended church family, but the real unconditional love from a real man. In her forty-six years of living, Mecia had only given her love to two men. Jax's father when she was young and wild. Then to Kam, Ke' and Marcus' father later down the line as she matured.

Unfortunately for her, neither of those men were around anymore. Jax's father was a man who broke her to the point where she thought she'd never love again. That was, until five years later when she met Kevin, who would become her first husband and father her youngest children. Their relationship wasn't without fault, but it was a promising marriage nonetheless. A marriage that lasted until Kevin's death did them part. When Marcus was just a baby, God called Kevin home without fair warning and since then, Mecia had been alone.

Pushing away further thoughts of discomfort, Mecia grabbed the now full pot and poured herself a healthy mug of her favorite blend. She took a second to make a snack, then found her way to the living room.

Mecia turned on the TV and scrolled through the channels, searching for one of the popular daytime soap operas that ruled mid-day television across the nation. In the back of her mind, she couldn't stop thinking of her youngest child. Since she gave him a hug and a kiss goodbye that morning, an eerie feeling attached itself to her gut.

She was still flicking through channels when her eyes caught a glimpse of a chaotic scene unfolding on the news channel. The reporter seemed to be delivering some tragic news as the camera panned around and zoomed in on a very familiar-looking silver Maserati.

Mecia's breathing slowed to slower intervals and her already abnormal heart began to tap dance. Now without a doubt, she saw exactly what had her feeling uneasy. As she timidly increased the volume, her heart broke…

"We have some breaking news on a shooting that took place earlier this morning near Texas Tech University. Here's reporter Gabrielle Rene' with more details on this developing story. Gabrielle…" the news anchorman said.

"Thanks, Ben… I'm here on the scene located at the corner of 19th and N. University, where something tragic has occurred. I've been informed by authorities that after an early morning run-in with a double homicide suspect, shots were fired that ultimately resulted in the suspect's death. The law enforcement officer involved in this deadly shooting is decorated detective, Samuel Sullivan. He claims to have received an anonymous tip giving him specific details on the murder suspect's whereabouts. Sullivan has stated that he spotted the suspect in traffic and attempted to conduct a routine stop, in hopes of bringing the suspect in for questioning. It was during this brief stop, that when asked to provide his license and registration, the suspect attempted to produce an automatic weapon from somewhere within the vehicle. A weapon he may have used to inflict harm or even kill Detective Sullivan.

"It's being said that the detective in question was fearful of his life and opened fire in his defense, which resulted in the suspect's death. The authorities here on the scene have recovered a weapon from the suspect's vehicle, which gave merit to Detective Sullivan's claim. They have positively identified the deceased male suspect as eighteen-year-old Marcus Cook. Cook was a recent commit to the Texas Tech University football program and it's being reported that he was actually enroute to his first practice before this incident occurred. Now, there are plenty of questions surrounding this case already and LPD's Police Chief Doyle has made it clear there will be a thorough investigation conducted on this matter. Either way, if this shooting is found to be justified or unjustified, this will mark the sixth police shooting of a black male this year alone. The city of Lubbock is still in an uproar over the murder of LPD Officer Brian Todd, so the attention this case will receive on a national level will be one for the books. At the moment, this is all the information I have been able to gather. I will give updates as they roll in. Thanks for watching. This is Gabrielle Rene', reporting for *KLBK Channel 13 News*. Back to you, Ben."

STEPHEN AND JAX sat inside room 3 of Studio 806, hard at work. They were busy mixing and mastering 3BG's latest cut with the City Girls. Interrupting the session, Jax's phone went off, loudly alerting him of a newly received text. What he read next would hurt him deeply, but sadly, it wouldn't be the worst news of the day.

When Jax first saw the name flash menacingly across the screen, he almost ignored the untimely text. It was an odd time for Cori to be trying to contact him. Especially after their last conversation. Still, he opened the message and read what she had to say.

Cori: "So… as you're reading this, I bet you're thinking, Damn, what this bitch want? Am I right? I know I am, ha-ha. Anyway, to answer your question, this 'BITCH' wants you to hurt! No, I don't mean physical pain or harm. That would be too easy. I mean heartache and emotional trauma, ya know? Why, you ask? Because after all the pain you have caused me, shit nigga, ya deserve it! I sat there and endured all that pain during Jr's labor only to have you basically abandon us. And for what? All cause of one stupid ass mistake I made in high school! We were both young and dumb back then... Anyway, your treatment of me over the years has made me resent you. I hate you and wish nothing but the worst for you. Since you clearly no longer care for me, you won't have to worry about me OR Jr. anymore. You will NEVER see him again! Now, before you pipe up and get all macho, just know as you're reading this, me and Jr. are far, far away from lil ole' Lubbock fuckin' Texas. Lol, you'd never guess where we are! I have plenty of money to live off of thanks to your friend now, so that money you used to send... keep it! Well, I think I've said enough... Goodbye, Jax!" The vindictive text finally ended.

Jax lifted his eyes from the screen. The rage that followed was instant.

"Man, what the fuck?" Jax busted out. "Nigga, this hoe trippin'! She done lost her muthafuckin' mind if she think she just finna—" His rant was cut short when his assistant LaKesha came running through the door, looking like hell.

LaKesha was a longtime family friend and somewhat of an aunt to Jax. He knew her well enough, and the look plastered over her face spoke volumes. Before she could say what, Jax already knew something was terribly wrong. Cori and Jr. popped into his mind first.

Stephen paused the thudding music so LaKesha's distraught voice could be heard.

"Oh my God! Oh my God! Jax! Hurry, turn on the news. It's Marcus, I can't believe what they are saying about Marcus!" she cried out.

Reacting without question, Jax quickly backed away from the computer monitors and sound boards in front of him. Frantically, he searched for the remote in the junk-food-ridden studio. When he found it and pressed the power button, he was devastated and rocked to his core with unfathomable grief.

CHAPTER 3
YOU'VE GOT TO BE FUCKIN' KIDDING

Just as Terry was pulling into Jax's designated parking space, he saw Jax rushing out of Studio 806's doors, with Kam hot on his heels.

The look written on his face was a clear indication that something was wrong, and the usually glamorous Kam looked as if someone had just announced the world was coming to an end. Her tears ruined her once flawlessly beat face and she moved frantically to try and keep pace with Jax.

Another boiling wave of disappointment washed over Terry when he saw the two. He knew for certain they had to have learned the news about Marcus by now and he was fucked up that he wasn't present to see the priceless looks of pain on their faces firsthand. "Fuck!" he cursed under his breath as he exited Jax's car. He was beyond upset that he missed the highlight of his day.

Thanks to Jax though, he would have his second chance to be near when more bad news was delivered. All he had to do was be patient and wait for Mecia's "new" meds to take effect. Terry had been plotting for six years on his revenge, so if he was anything, he was patient.

"Wassup Jax, man? Everything aight, my nigga?" Terry said as he approached Jax in front of the studio entrance, tossing his key back to him.

"T.J., hold it down with Stephen till I get back, I gotta run... Family emergency," Jax explained as he quickly brushed past Terry. His response seemed a bit rude, given the level of concern Terry showed, but at the moment he didn't give one fuck.

Jax and Kam jumped in the car and then for the second time in only an hour that day, Jax's Bugatti was again pushed to its limits as he peeled out the parking lot in a desperate attempt to save a brother that couldn't be saved.

———

FOR WHATEVER REASON, KE' just wasn't feeling class that day and decided to take a much needed half-day. She always had perfect attendance and kept her grades up in every course, so she figured she could afford to play hooky one time.

That morning had already been so chaotic anyway, no one would probably notice her absence. The entire campus was crawling with cops, camera crews and reporters all in a frenzy for the inside scoop on a shooting that took place earlier that morning within walking distance of the campus.

Not being super nosey like her peers, Ke' was completely out of the loop on what had actually taken place. She had absolutely no idea her little brother had tragically lost his life at the hectic crime scene she'd just passed.

Unlike any of her flashy siblings, Ke' was quite simple. She didn't push a foreign like them, she cruised in a modest

VW Beetle. Relaxing a bit, Ke' cut up the music and sang her lil heart out along with the voice of another Lubbock artist by the name of LOVE. Ke' wasn't the best singer in the family, but she made up for what she lacked vocally with her amazing dance skills.

Since she was already out and about, she decided to head up to the studio with her fam and hang out for a while. While there, she planned to pitch Jax some new ideas for the upcoming video shoots.

Once Ke' arrived, she noticed Jax's car was gone but Kam's Range Rover was still there, so she got out and headed inside.

Terry just kind of milled around the studio with Stephen, not really sure what to do. He wasn't in the mood to work, and neither was Stephen. Stephe was quite fond of Marcus, seeing how he watched the kid grow over the years. The sudden news of his death really hit him hard too.

"Aye man, I'ma step outside for some fresh air and a smoke break," Terry said to Stephen as he left out of room 3.

So far, Terry's plan for revenge was going according to plan, but Marcus' death was a bittersweet victory. He would die to see the look on Jax's face right now…

More luck seemed to shower Terry as he stepped outside. His heart skipped a beat when his eyes met Ke's. He knew when they first met, they had chemistry. It was an instant connection that couldn't be missed. They just never got the chance to really speak on it.

The smile on her face, the flow of her hair and the sway of her hips captivated him, and he knew then this was his moment, his best chance to get her. Although Terry was young, he was well aware that a vulnerable woman was easy pickings. What could possibly make a young woman like

Ke' more vulnerable than learning of the death of a loved one?

Terry would be sure she had a shoulder to cry on when he softly broke the news. *Being there for her during a time like this would surely grant him more time with her in the future, wouldn't it?* Terry thought.

———

SECONDS after the horrifying news segment ended, the phone in Mecia's hands rang. Without thought, she answered it, still in a state of shock. The voice on the other end of the phone was soft but straight forward in her delivery. The voice simply stated her reason for calling was because Mecia's presence was needed immediately down at the city morgue to identify the remains of a young male presumed to be her son, Marcus Cook.

Before the woman could finish her request, Mecia sprang to her feet and darted to her bedroom. She threw on random clothing articles and it looked as if she'd dressed herself in the dark, but at that moment, she gave less than a damn about her physical appearance.

Her heart and mind were only on Marcus and what could have possibly gone wrong. She had just kissed her youngest child goodbye hours ago as he left for college, and now all of a sudden, the news was reporting him dead. And not just dead, he had been shot, murdered. In Mecia's eyes it couldn't be true. She prayed to God Almighty it wasn't…

———

JAX AND KAM weaved in and out of traffic, speeding downtown. He was all too familiar with death, given the amount he'd seen over the years, some of it even at his own hands. But in no way was he ready for this shit. Especially after the loss of D. Lee and Greedy B.

He knew if the reports turned out to be true, Marcus' body would be taken to the city morgue and held until a positive identification had been made by a family member.

The last time Jax had spoken to his mother, she said she was going to take a nap. He hoped like hell she was still asleep. This news would kill her and that would kill him.

Jax racked his brain, trying to come to a conclusion on what could have led to such a tragedy. News reports claimed Marcus was shot during a traffic stop and that just wasn't making any fuckin' sense to Jax.

As he pulled into the morgue's parking lot, his heart skipped two beats. A sparkling purple E-Class Mercedes Benz was parked crooked in the emergency space with the engine still running. He'd bought the car for Mecia a few Christmases back and knew for a fact it was the only one like it in the city. So, that meant his mother definitely wasn't still napping. There was no way he would be able to shield her from this. That thought alone broke his heart. He could only imagine what it would do to hers.

———

MECIA'S NERVES WERE SHOT, and she was in a fit of tears. Her eyes were filled with liquid sadness like two watery pools of woe as dread grew from deep within her soul. She stifled a small shudder as she watched the emotionless coroner open a refrigerated cabinet and slide out a cold, metallic slab with a low pressurized hiss, followed by a faint cloud of foggy air.

Draped in a heavenly white sheet, lie a huge corpse with the sort of stillness only death could provide.

More pain crept into Mecia's chest, threatening to steal every breath in her frail body. Her anxiety raced and her legs shook profusely, on the verge of betraying her balance.

Two pairs of strong and warm, consoling hands graced her shoulders in a comforting fashion as Jax and Kam appeared next to her, offering their support. All three of them were silent as the graveyard as they awaited the moment of truth.

The coroner grabbed the corner of the folds of the sheet that covered the morgue's newest guest. He seemed so emotionally withdrawn. Truth be told, he hated this part of his job. It hurt him deeply every time he had to reveal a body to a grieving family. Sometimes he felt as though he had very well snuffed the victim's life away himself. He took a deep breath as he felt the family's chilling stares through the window. With the slightest head nod from Jax as nonverbal approval, he removed the sheet.

Despite the violent way Marcus perished, he laid on that stainless steel slab with a peaceful look that made everyone uneasy. The sight of him lying there lifeless crushed the family and they all began to sob.

"Oh, Lord! Not my baby!" Mecia wept. "Not my babyyy!"

"No, God. My baby brother's gone! Wh-what the hell happened?" Kam screamed. She was irate and completely overcome with raw, uncut emotion.

Jax was stuck. He couldn't believe his eyes. He wasn't ready to accept the harsh truth. On his way down to the morgue, he was so sure there had been a mistake. While behind the wheel of his car, he did something he hadn't done in a while... he prayed.

He asked God over and over to please spare the life of his only brother. Jax literally begged for some mercy, but it was clear that his prayers went unanswered.

Blue blood boiled in his veins and a side of him he always kept suppressed around his family began to make headway. Quickly, his calculated, professional demeanor began to fade. The blow was simply too much for him and he was losing it!

Mecia and Kam continued to wail uncontrollably, further making Jax's temper rise. His loved ones were hurting, and he couldn't do shit about it. Suddenly, he thought about Ke'. She would surely take the news pretty hard too...

"Fuck!" Jax let out between clenched teeth. His baby brother was dead. Like really dead. He needed answers and fast. *Somebody somewhere was gonna pay for this shit.* Retaliation was the only thing on his mind, regardless of the reprimands that may come with it.

Before the family could even fully process their loss and grief, they were approached by a black man in a suit.

The man was none other than Detective B. Crockette. He was one of the only three African American males working within the LPD. Both he and Jax had a lot more in common than either of them knew at the time.

Aware of the shocking news the family had just received, the detective approached with caution and treaded lightly. He was there to conduct a follow-up investigation into Marcus' death and interview the family as requested by his LPD superiors and another very powerful man he answered to.

"Excuse me," he spoke to the family lightly. "My name is Detective Crockette, I assume you three are the family of the deceased?"

Trying his best to muster some form of calmness, Jax turned to the detective and said, "Correct." Mecia and Kam kept crying.

Sensing the family's curiosity and obvious agitation, he got right to the point, knowing what questions they were bound to ask.

"I know this... uh, this situation is extremely painful and quite difficult to understand or accept. I want to start by saying I'm genuinely sorry for your loss and I personally don't like the way things have transpired. I reassure you I'm doing my best to get to the bottom of this. It may take time, but I will get to the bottom of this entire ordeal surrounding Marcus' death. I believe I was chosen to lead this investigation due to the extreme circumstances, as well as the underlying racial factors in this case. I'm not positive if race or anything of that nature will be an issue in this matter, but I swear to perform a thorough investigation. Now, in order for me to do so, I will need full cooperation from all three of you," Detective Crockette made himself clear.

The last part of the detective's speech didn't sit well with Jax. He wasn't the type to cooperate with law enforcement in any way for various reasons. For one, he didn't trust any of them muthafuckas for shit! Two, he didn't want to run the risk of ever popping up on their radar. And three, the crooked muthafuckas had a hard time doing their job, even when you were cooperative. But his little brother was dead. Murdered by a cop, so this made shit different and Jax was more than uncomfortable.

Though the brisk sniffles, Mecia spoke up. "Sir, we are all willing to help in any way possible. I just want to know what happened to my baby. Please tell me why my son—" another fit of tears took over.

"Well, ma'am, nothings clear at this point in the investigation. But it's being said that the LPD was showing interest in Marcus as a prime suspect for a double homicide that took place earlier this month at a club called Snow City." Detective Crockett flipped through his notes. " Says here the victims were one Bryon Parker and DeMarco Lee—"

"What the fuck? Man, hell nah! That's a muthafuckin' lie. Ain't no way in hell my brother did no shit like that. Police ain't had no leads for weeks. I even put a hundred-thousand-dollar reward out for info and ain't nobody sayin' shit. Now all of a sudden, y'all gone pin some shit like this on him to cover y'all asses... This some bullshit!" Jax flew off the handle.

Crockett remained calm. "Sir, like I said, nothing is exactly clear on the matter yet. I can only relay to you what is being said until my investigation is complete to my standards."

"Well, what the fuck else is being said?" Jax questioned, his fury quite apparent.

"Unfortunately, there was a weapon recovered at the scene from Marcus' vehicle, which was a silver Maserati, I believe."

"Whoa, whoa, there's no way my baby had a gun, sir. You don't understand. He was on his way to college. Today was his first day, he-he wouldn't..." Mecia's chest began to ache. She was overwhelming herself. "How's this even possible?"

"As far as I know at the moment, Marcus was stopped in traffic today by an off-duty detective, who received an inside tip on Marcus' whereabouts. During the stop, when asked to present his ID and registration etc., Marcus 'allegedly' attempted to withdraw the weapon from the vehicle's glove compartment. What his intentions were or would have been are unknown, but to ensure his own safety, the detective opened fire which resulted in Marcus' death." Telling the family this, Detective Crockette could see the look of horror on Mecia's face. "Again, ma'am, I am truly sorry for your loss," he reiterated.

Mecia and Kam were stunned into silence and total disbelief. These actions were beyond Marcus' character. Shooting a cop was something they just couldn't fathom him doing under any circumstances. They knew it wasn't true, no way, no how. There was definitely some bullshit in the game somewhere.

"Listen, I hate to say this, but the worst part of this all is…" the detective looked each of them in the eye before he continued, "The police put a rush on the ballistics and weapons testing when the gun was recovered and about an hour ago the results came in. The weapon recovered today from Marcus' vehicle, with his prints on it, is a hundred percent match to the weapon that killed those two young men at Snow City."

"You've got to be fuckin' kidding me! My brother wasn't even at that fuckin' party. He was at home watchin' film. He don't know shit 'bout no guns. Man, this shit is crazy!" Jax exclaimed.

"I really wish this evidence weren't true," Detective Crockette sympathized.

"What's the detective's name who did this shit?" Jax pointed toward the glass window. "Somethin' ain't right! I know for a fact Marcus ain't do no shit like that. Greedy and D. Lee were my brothers too! Marcus loved and looked up to them, just like he did me."

"The involved detective's name is Samuel Sullivan. He is currently down at headquarters pending the outcome of this investigation."

"Well, I'ma let you know one thing, Detective," Jax stated

boldly, "y'all police muthafuckas better figure this shit out quick! It's obvious that crooked cop outright murdered my brother in cold blood! Anyone who knew Marcus knows damn well he wasn't capable of doing the shit y'all claim. I'm tellin' you now, if that bastard walks free on this shit, it won't be long before he's the one being mourned!" Jax said his piece and stormed off. All hell was sure to break loose soon. The city of Lubbock would rain red if Jax found out how deep this shit went.

Jax was crazy, but his uncle Big D was a damn lunatic! The death of his nephew was gonna make him trip the fuck out. Especially when he found out who did it…

CHAPTER 4

I GOT YOU BABE

Jax managed to finally get himself, Mecia and Kam away from the detective and out of the morgue without tearing the place up. All of them were livid and short on understanding at the time.

Mecia's heart was broken. She was doing her best to cope and handle the situation, but the main organ in her body didn't agree. Her chest tightened and she started to feel real weak, experiencing shortness of breath. Jax noticed her condition on the walk outside as it dawned on him a dose of her meds would be helpful. Luckily, they were in his car, courtesy of Terry's trip to the pharmacy.

Quickly, Jax fed Mecia a capsule and saw her relax a bit as it traveled its course through her body. It would help temporarily, but nothing short of Marcus' resurrection could heal her pain. She didn't know what to do, her youngest son was dead and her oldest looked ready to kill. That day she'd seen a brief glimpse of the character she heard he could turn into years ago and it scared her half to death. Crazy part about it, Jax held it together for the most part. She could only imagine if he lost control. Was he making idle threats? Was she in danger of losing him too? Her heart couldn't take that.

"Kam, I know you came up here with me, but I think it'd be best if you drove Ma home, she ain't lookin' so good. I'll meet y'all at the house later," Jax stated.

Kam silently nodded in agreement.

"Jax please don't do anything stupid, son. Don't make this any worse," Mecia pleaded.

"I won't, Ma. I just need some time to look into all this and see what's really going on. I'll be by the house later. Kam, just make sure she gets some rest and if Ke' comes by before I get there, please break the news to her gently. And make sure she's sitting down first. You know how she is and how fragile her emotions can be. I'd much rather y'all wait till I get back to tell her, though."

Again, Kam only nodded. She couldn't think straight enough to speak.

To avoid making his mother any promises he couldn't keep, Jax left quickly. Mecia's look said she wanted further confirmation he wasn't going to wild out, and he just couldn't give that to her now!

———

"WELL, HELLO STRANGER, HOW ARE YOU?" Ke' asked Terry. He was coming out of the studio as she was heading in.

"I'm good. How are you, beautiful?" Terry responded with natural charm. He reached to shake her hand and maybe even kiss her wrist, but Ke' was too friendly for handshakes.

"It's nice to see you again," she said with open arms, blushing uncontrollably.

Seeing the invitation for a hug, Terry obliged. Engulfed in

her arms, he wrapped his arms around her slender frame, pulling her closer. Her bosom met his chest, and the aroma of her sweet-scented perfume tickled his nostrils.

"It's really nice to see you again too," Terry said as they began to distance themselves.

A moment of clarity passed between them as they locked eyes, holding each other's hands at arm's length. It was obvious they were feeling each other without either one of them having to say so or even knowing much of each other.

"So, why the long face?" Ke' asked.

"Uh, just getting some fresh air and trying to clear my mind with everything that's going on today," Terry reeled her in.

"What's going on? Anything I can help you with?" Ke' asked with concern. She didn't know what it was about him, but she liked Terry and wanted to be around him more.

Sensing the opportunity drawing nearer, Terry went for the kill.

"Ke', I hate to dampen the mood and kill whatever it is we got goin, but I assume you haven't heard the news yet, huh?"

"What news?"

"You mean, your family hasn't called you yet?"

"No, why? Is everything okay?" Ke' questioned, the worry in her voice evident.

"Ke', I really don't want to be the bearer of such bad news," Terry told her, "I think you need to get up with your peoples, like ASAP!"

"Is Jax here?" Ke' asked, scanning the lot once again for his car.

"Nah, him and Kam rushed out of here not long ago."

"What? Tell me what's going on! Is everyone okay?

Please tell me what happened." Ke' clenched one hand harder and ran the other over her gelled baby hair nervously.

"It's Marcus," Terry revealed.

"Marcus? What about him? Did he get in some kind of trouble or something?" Ke' rattled off questions left and right.

Terry was silent, purposely letting the suspense of the unknown for Ke' build. As intended, the lack of Terry's response to her questioning began to give Ke' the coldest chills. Not knowing what was going on was quickly eating away at her.

"Please tell me my brother is okay. Where is he?"

"Ke'... I'm sorry to tell you this, but Marcus is dead!" Before Terry could say more, Ke' fainted. She collapsed suddenly into Terry's arms.

Holding her in his grasp, Terry knew he had her. True, her heart would be broken when she regained full consciousness and realized this wasn't a dream but an actual nightmare. Terry was now in a position to be there to help Ke' heal. His plan was still rolling without a hitch. So, he would be ready for the next step. It was sure to crush Jax even more and draw Ke' even closer than she already was.

————

"DOMINO, MUTHAFUCKA!" BIG D yelled, as he viciously slammed the black and white ceramic domino against the clothed steel table. "Ha-ha-ha," he laughed evilly. "Gon' rise up, nigga. Who got next drop?"

BIG D was full of that Colombian coffee, zu-zu's, wham-whams, shit talk and good humor. This was his daily norm during day room hours when he got together with his fellow gamblers and played a penitentiary Domino game called Knock.

He was by far the best player on the unit, credited to his sixteen years of experience and intimate knowledge of numbers and how they worked.

"Man, goddamn! Y'all can't hold this nigga or what?" Mike complained. He was the guy in BIG D's circle of hustlas who was always losing. Yet and still, he continued to play anyway just to chill and pass time with the crew.

BIG D was already up a few dollars and more than likely would have run Mike, Shitty Loc and Champ further in the hole, but suddenly his name was called over the cell block's PA system.

"Derrick Cook, please report to the chaplain's office. Cook to the chaplain's office," a womanly robotic-like voice commanded over the intercom.

An instant look of apprehension plastered the face of everyone at the table, especially BIG D's. Everybody knew that unless you worked for the chaplain, being called down to his office out of the blue was never a good thing. It could only be for one or two reasons. Either one of your family members was deathly ill and wanted you notified, or in the worst case they were already dead. The prison systems often used the chaplain to deliver harsh news as such, with hopes that the chaplain, being a man of faith and great understanding would help soften the blow about to be untimely delivered.

Damn, I wonder what the fuck's going on? BIG D thought over and over on his way to the chaplain.

A million different scenarios formed in his mind all at once and he wasn't ready to handle any of them. This was the part of prison he hated the most. The lack of control he had in certain situations like this one made him feel uneasy. Without even speaking to the chaplain yet, he was sure something was terribly wrong with one of his loved ones. And it hurt to know there was nothing he could do about it. Aware of Mecia's sometimes fragile condition, he automatically assumed the worst…

The news he received about his nephew Marcus moments later tore what was left of his heart in two. Marcus' promising life was taken away by the hands of the people BIG D despised the most, the LPD.

It was more than ironic that Marcus' death wasn't at the hand of some random officer, but by BIG D's worst enemy. A man he loathed in every way… Detective Samuel Sullivan!

BIG D never really gave a fuck about or regretted anything he'd ever done. Not even fuckin' with Vivian's snake ass. But now with Marcus' death on his conscience, he regretted killing Detective Sullivan's wife all those years ago in that courtroom.

Nancy Sullivan was a power-abusing, wicked racist woman, who took the precious lives of many minorities and eventually got what she deserved. But BIG D never once thought taking her life would result in him losing one of his own family members.

The anger that developed within him upon hearing this shocking news was immediate. His whole body was over-dosed with gentrified rage!

Swiftly, BIG D made it back to the privacy of his cell and sat in agonizing silence. Mentally, he was about to lose it and desperately tried to calm himself. He felt the overwhelming need to settle the score with his rival, but the eternal confine-ment of the federal institution he resided in wouldn't allow the retribution he craved.

As a single tear made a great escape from the corner of his

grief-stricken brown eyes, BIG D caught a glimpse of the woman he'd grown to love standing quietly in the doorway of his cell. He had the kind of love for Angela he never thought he could give to any woman outside of Tina.

Time after time, she constantly proved to be worthy of a permanent place in his heart. Being the strong, alpha male he was, BIG D didn't want her to witness his current emotional state. Due to Angela having multiple connections both in and outside of the prison, she'd learned of Marcus' death rather quickly. Marcus and Angela had never once met, but she considered him family because of her undying love for BIG D. So, the loss hurt her too.

When she was informed of the circumstances surrounding Marcus and found out who actually killed him, her stomach churned with disgust. The hate she held for Samuel Sullivan ran deep just off the strength of her relationship with BIG D. Now this situation only made it worse. It made her want to kill the man her damn self, but she wouldn't dare deprive BIG D of that honor.

That morning, Angela made a long overdue visit to the institution's doctor's office. As she'd done ever so slightly over the years, she flirted with the old white man, stroking his ego and his inner thigh until he was like putty in her hands. With perfect timing, she finally had him right where she wanted him.

In no time, Angela would get what she wanted from him. BIG D's freedom was well worth the price she was set to pay. Angela was beyond beautiful, with a body that defied her age and would generate lustful thoughts from any man. One dose of her and she'd easily become a man's obsession. This would be the case for sixty-year-old, Doctor Clayton Carson.

The old man was a loveless loner, and would do anything

to have a piece of Angela. Even if only for one night. He'd finally tired of the depression that gripped him for years after his wife left him for a much younger, richer guy.

Dr. Carson had no children, habits or hobbies, which only made him drown himself in work and take his job too serious. Way too serious. But he was still a man. A man with many desires. A man with needs! He had many explicit fantasies and fetishes, and Angela had promised to fulfill all of them. For one *big* favor of course.

Entering BIG D's cell, Angela knew he had already heard the news by his demeanor and the tears that now freely cascaded down his deep brown face. She was so in love with BIG D and wanted nothing more than for him to be happy. Easing closer to him, she reached out and began to caress his tense, knotted shoulders.

"Baby, I'm so sorry for your loss," she spoke tenderly.

Without response, BIG D fell back and leaned his heavy head into the softness of her chest as she rubbed his pounding heart. "I know we've talked about trying to get ya out of here for years and now I think this is the perfect time. I have a date with Doctor Carson tonight and I'll get him to go along with our plan. Baby, I know you're hurting, and I know exactly what will make you feel better, cause I know you. Within the next week or so, revenge will be yours and I'll be right by your side. The Bonnie to your Clyde. Trust me when I say I got you, babe!"

Nothing else needed to be said. Absolutely forgetting where they were or just simply not caring anymore, she began to kiss him sensually as her manicured hands roamed over his blood-filled dick. Even mourning his nephew's death couldn't put a pause to the sexual reaction Angela could create when she touched him.

Pulling him out to full length, Angela expertly took all of him in her mouth, deep throating him as she loved to do. She even managed to give his balls a lick or two with a sexually curled tongue, while staring into his watery eyes. Lovingly, Angela put forth her best efforts to orally heal him and literally suck the pain away.

Soon, BIG D would be free! If only Samuel Sullivan knew what he had coming...

CHAPTER 5

A FAVOR FOR A FAVOR

"Somebody tell me why/ Why the good die young/ Sometimes it makes me cry, cry/ To know that your gone/ I'll hold on to your memories/ Not a day goes by/ I hear a voice say dry those eyes/ Cause real niggas never die!" The melodic voice of Cee Lo Green pumped through Jax's speakers. The song called "Never Die," featuring the late great Nipsey Hu$$le, spoke his true feelings.

Jax was fucked up! His emotions teetered constantly from cry to kill. He didn't know what to do with himself. Needing answers and some comfort, he decided to go visit D. Lee and Greedy.

The thought that Marcus would soon be in the ground right next to them really broke his heart. A broken-hearted man could be dangerous!

———

SELFISHLY, TERRY DIDN'T WANT KE' to awaken. She was undeniably gorgeous and fit so perfectly into the contours of his chiseled arms. He didn't expect her to faint the way she had after hearing the news of her brother's death. But in a rather twisted way, he was glad she did, assuming that would initiate a bond between them and make it easier to court her.

When Ke' stirred from her unconscious state and her hazelish-colored eyes opened up, Terry cleared the lustrous hair from her slightly perspired face and held her gaze. Trying to fully come to, she attempted to sit up quickly, but Terry's soft words and firm grip around her gave her pause.

"It's going to be okay. I got you. I'll help ya through this," Terry promised.

"What happened? Why am I on the ground?" Ke' asked to shake the confusion.

"Uh, well, I-I was trying to explain what happened to Marcus and when I did, you-you..." Terry stuttered.

He didn't have to complete his sentence for Ke' to understand the gravity of what had taken place. She knew she fainted. For some reason, that was always her reaction to immense pressure or devastating news. Terry's revelation was slowly coming back to her.

"I'm sorry," she said weakly.

"Shh, it's not your fault," Terry assured her as he looked into her eyes and cupped her chin sweetly.

"M-my brother, he's—" Ke's eyes began to water as she tried to get the words out.

"He's in a better place now. Come on, let's get up and get you to your family. Y'all need each other right now."

Terry helped Ke' up and over to her vehicle. He took matters into his own hands since he was aware of the traumatic state she was still in. Terry carefully guided her into the passenger seat and drove her home.

He'd already been to her mother's home with Jax not too long ago, so he knew exactly where to go.

Ke' sat in the passenger seat, restrained by the seat belt, staring out the window as Terry drove. So much weighed on her mental. *What exactly had happened to Marcus*? How was her family taking the news? Was her mother okay? Questions upon questions invaded her conscience. She constantly wiped her eyes.

Halfway to their destination, Terry's phone rang. Only two people had this number, considering he just got the phone and didn't deal with many people. He answered on the second ring and steered with one hand.

"Hello?" Terry said into the phone as he snuck a side glance over to Ke', who was still disengaged from reality.

"Terry! I'm gonna need that favor a lot sooner than later. I can't do this anymore… She's doing it again! Brother, please —" Tory broke down. "Please help me!"

"I'm in the middle of something right now. Give me an hour and I promise I'll be there to take care of your problem. Just please hang on and stall her out as long as you can. Send me the address and stay alert," Terry ordered.

"Okay," Tory sniffled and reluctantly disconnected the call. She hoped like hell she could count on her long-lost twin to come and liberate her from what seemed to be eternal sexual torment.

————

NOT LONG AFTER the call ended, Terry pulled into Mecia's driveway and parked behind her sparkling purple Benz. As a true gentleman should, Terry exited her car first and went over to the passenger side, proceeding to help Ke' out and walk to the front door of the house.

Making it to the porch, Terry decided to shoot his shot at Ke', despite the circumstances.

"Uh... look, Ke', please don't take this the wrong way, but I was wondering if I could have your number. I know this is really bad timing, but I really just want to be here for you if ya need someone. I know how it feels to lose a brother."

Before Ke' could find the words to say to Terry, the dead-bolt security locks on the front door made their heads turn.

Kam appeared in the doorway with a twisted look on her tear-stained face and folded arms. Her dislike for Terry was clear since day one and on this day it would be no different.

"Excuse me, what's going on here?" Kam sounded motherly.

"I was just bringing Ke' home. Uh, she came by the studio right after you and Jax left and when she heard about Marcus, she—"

"Marcus!" Kam's eyes grew wide and lit up with fire. "Muthafucka, you told her?" she yelled.

"Well... yeah, I thought she had the right to know what was going on. I mean, it is her brother too," Terry argued. It was so hard for him to hide his attitude towards her. Kam always fucked with him for no reason and just rudely interfered with the game he was laying on her sister.

"Nigga, ya had no goddamn right to open you mouth about our business! You—" Kam was 'bout to go in on Terry before Ke' cut her off.

"Kam, chill please! He was only trying to help me. Everything is okay," Ke' said as she eyed a tight-jawed Terry.

"Ke', can't you see everything is not okay? Shit! Our baby brother's gone... Gone! And this nigga tryna relay information like he just know some shit. This is a tragic moment for our family and he has the nerve to be lookin' at you with lust in his eyes." Kam's words dripped venom as she continued her trip.

"Enough, Kam! Like I said already, he was only trying to help. You can't sit here and take your anger out on him. It's not like he had anything to do with it. You are out of line and ya should apologize to him," Ke' said as she folded her arms and matched Kam's glare.

Snaking her neck, Kam yelled, "I wish the fuck I would!" then rolled her eyes and stormed off.

Ke' turned back to Terry. "I'm so sorry. You have to forgive my sister, she can be so... so Kam!"

"It's okay. I understand death affects everyone different-ly," Terry responded. "Well, I'ma get out of here and let ya get in there to your family. I'm sure they need you now."

"Yeah, you're right. I guess I'll see you around," Ke' said as she turned to enter the house.

Terry watched her briefly, then turned to leave before Ke's voice caught his attention.

"Hey! Uh, don't you still want my number?"

Before he could say yes fast enough, Ke' stepped to him, took the initiative and stuck her hand in the front pocket of his pants and retrieved his phone swiftly. Her finger glided across the screen, entering her digits at lightning speed. She snuck a glance at Terry's approving face and offered the best smile he could muster.

"Stay in touch," Ke' said and gave Terry a small peck on his cheek. Then she disappeared into the house.

Walking away from the porch, Terry made sure to save her info, then he went to his Uber App and summoned a ride, since he'd abandoned Lil Vicc's Lexus at the studio in order to bring Ke' home. He waited the full six minutes it took for the Uber driver to arrive and left with a big smile on his face.

———

THE ESTIMATED DRIVE ahead was a little over thirty minutes, to a city called Levelland, TX. So he only had half an hour to concoct a viable plan to punish this Les character for the cruel acts she'd committed against his only sister. Terry didn't have his MP5 with him, but he did carry a small .22 he found in Lil Vicc's room. The weapon wasn't nearly as intimidating as the MP5 was, but it would have to get the job done. Terry wasn't sure exactly what he was gonna do though. He was just gonna wing it.

Right on time, he arrived in a lavish gated community. The homes were nice, all resembling each other in one way or another and gave off a rich vibe.

Damn, sis out here living the good life! Terry thought dumbly. He soon remembered the horror in Tory's eyes as she recounted all the things she'd dealt with since a child. Terry realized at that point, everything is not always what it seems.

"Stop right here," he told the driver. He was a few houses away from Tory's house when he tipped the driver and got out. Terry walked briskly toward the address he received and knew he was at the correct house when he saw the same truck he admired outside the pharmacy. When Tory sent him the address, she told him the door would be open. Not knowing what to expect on the inside, Terry pulled out the .22 and entered the marvelous home with caution.

———

ACROSS THE STREET, Tina was on speakerphone with BIG D while she stood in the kitchen, in front of the sink doing dishes. BIG D's voice came through the phone, telling her a lot of things she hoped to be true and some she wished were not true at all.

Looking up through the window for a second, she noticed a young looking guy clad in street clothes that caught her attention when he entered the house across from her with a small gun in hand.

"Uh, baby," Tina said wearily. "I think Les has some unexpected company!"

———

THE INSIDE of the home took Terry by surprise. It was elegant, massive and stocked with expensive material items. Silence filled the home, save for the faint traces of sound coming from somewhere upstairs. It sounded like muffled moans of pleasure, or maybe it was pain?

Terry gripped the .22 tighter and began to climb up the swirling stairs.

Smack! The sound echoed throughout the master bedroom as Les' open hand collided with Tory's pretty face. No matter how many times this happened, Tory could never get used to it.

"Now, why don't you be a good girl like I said, and assume the fuckin' position! No back talk. And don't you dare run from me! It will only make things worse… I'm surprised you're not used to this by now. You can fight it all you want, but you and I both know that I make ya feel good… don't I?"

"Les, please don't do this," Tory began to beg. Then Les

raised her hand like she was ready to strike again, so Tory did as she was told like an ever obedient child.

Les watched with pure fire and desire burning within her as Tory leaned back on the bed and propped herself up on the cushioned sex pillow as ordered. With all her nakedness exposed, Tory felt helpless as usual. Tory was a stunning sexy girl who favored the pop-star, Rihanna. With her bald, meaty pussy lips on full display and her clit slightly peeking from its hood, Les' mouth watered with sexual anticipation. Tory hated the despicable acts Les had forced her into over the years, robbing her of her sweet innocence as an adolescent. She really, really, hoped Terry was going to show up and help her. Especially since she did that favor for him.

Tory's legs were ajar, with her hips set at a slight incline, just how Les liked. As she'd done many times before, Les lowered her solid figure onto the bed and docked her face into the fresh scented depths of Tory's stallion-like thighs. Entrapping her with a strong grip on her child bearing hips, Tory had nowhere to run.

Les wasted no time and quickly latched onto Tory's swelling clitoris and went into a pussy eating frenzy, licking and sucking away. It was amazing to Les how Tory's mind always seemed to say no, but her body... her body sang a different song.

Only minutes into her feast, Les made Tory's body shake and was generously rewarded with her sweet bodily fluids.

Tory was ashamed. She hated the way her own body would betray her every single time. She couldn't deny the fact that Les' oral prowess felt amazing, but she didn't want it to. Tory knew it was wrong on so many levels and felt sick every time she felt those twisted waves of pleasure forced on her.

"Ooh, baby, you're sweeter than your mother ever was!" Les commented while licking her thick lips.

"Les, please—"

"Shh! No back talk, remember? We're not done yet. I got something special for your lil ass tonight," Les said with a certain smugness.

Tory had no clue what Les had up her sleeve and damn sure wasn't trying to find out. The time that elapsed since she spoke with Terry already seemed like a lifetime ago and she wondered if he was really coming for her. She looked down to the half-heart birthmark they shared and shed a tear.

―――――

FINALLY, Terry reached the third floor of the house. He was out of breath and his legs burned. There were three doors on the third floor of the house and Terry was unsure which one to open. He quietly approached the one on the right. It opened, led to an office of some sort. The second, a large bathroom. At the end of the hallway was a third door and once he made it within earshot, the sounds on the other side seemed to resemble those of pleasure, so he listened harder. He had no room for mistakes.

―――――

LES CAME out of her closet wielding a Louis Vuitton suitcase and placed it at the foot of the bed. As she unzipped the case, she smiled like the cat who caught the canary. The contents within were a lesbian's treasure trove. Sex toys flooded the inside. An assortment of oils, sex books and stimulant items intended for both pain and pleasure.

"Close your eyes," Les ordered.

Not one for confrontation, Tory obeyed. All she could hear was the sound of some kind of belt fastening and the jingling of small metallic buckles.

"Okay… open them," Les said.

Timidly, Tory eased her eyes open and damn near jumped out of her skin. Les was on her knees in front of her, stroking oil onto a huge life-like dildo that was strapped into a harness around her waist.

Fear claimed Tory's heart immediately. She'd never seen anything like it before. Believe it or not, unlike most girls her age, Tory was a virgin and had never participated in any sexual acts, outside of the oral sex forced on her by Les. She'd never been actually penetrated either, except for Les' probing finger every now and then. She thought for sure the size of that thing would kill her!

"I call him BIG BLACK. He was your mother's favorite," Les said, beaming with pride. "He's beautiful, huh?"

"I-I don't want to. Please… please, Les, don't! Don't make me," Tory whimpered, instinctively trying to back away from the perceived danger. Her attempt to flee lasted only a few seconds until she backed into the luxurious head-board. It seemed to reach out and bear hug her, holding her in place.

"What did I tell you about running from me?" Les admonished Tory smugly while the swollen, mushroom head of the dildo swung an unfathomable thirteen inches away from her waist. "Turn over… Now!"

"No! Please, don't—" Another powerful slap cut her plea short.

A strong thrust from Les and Tory was on her stomach. Face down, ass up! Tory turned her neck to the side to catch a breath and continue her plea bargain. "Les, please! I'm saving myself for marriage. Don't do this to me!"

Les didn't have the slightest care in the world for Tory's feelings. "Don't you worry your pretty little head. I'll save something for the idiot who marries you!" Les growled. Then with no further hesitation or warning, she reared back, gaining some strength and shoved the first six inches of BIG BLACK into uncharted territory.

———

TERRY HEARD the entire ordeal and it had him furious. Hearing his sister's pleas go in one ear and out the other made him lose it. He twisted the doorknob and it was locked. So, he walked back a few steps and ran full speed into the door, shoulder first, giving it all he had.

———

TORY DIDN'T KNOW what hurt worse, the immediate entry of the huge dildo inside her anus or the rapid exit of the endowment when Les jerked it out, after the bedroom door flew off the hinges. Les turned quickly to the sound and saw a man who looked identical to the woman below her. She was in a compromising position and in no way ready to react appropriately. Terry moved in her direction with the .22 held high. "Get the fuck off my sister, you sick bitch!" he yelled, landing a heavy blow to her forehead, with the butt of the small gun.

Les' body crumbled from the blow and landed on the floor with a resounding thud. She was knocked the fuck out, with BIG BLACK still towering from her harness.

The relief Tory felt at that moment was unreal. Her backside was on fire, but she could now deal with the pain. She covered herself with the sheets and began to weep, thanking Terry constantly.

"I told you I was coming, Sis! What, you didn't believe me?" Terry said. "Go get some clothes on. I think it's only fair she gets a taste of her own medicine!"

When Les woke up, her head throbbed, and she felt dizzy from the lick she took. Her hands and ankles were restrained in furry cuffs that prohibited much of her movement. She was now face down on the bed in a dooming position, with enough room to turn her head sideways. No way of knowing what was going on behind her, nor did she have the power to stop it. Les was terrified but tried not to show it.

"Tory! I swear to God if you don't get these goddamn cuffs off me, when I do get loose, I'ma fuck you up!" Les threatened.

"Who said you were gonna get loose again?" Terry toyed with her.

"Oh, hell nah! Tory! Who the fuck is that?" Les started trippin. "I know damn well you ain't got no nigga in my fuckin' house!" she yelled, struggling with the furry restraints. "Y'all better quit with the damn games and let me out of this shit right now!"

Smack! Tory delivered a thundering slap of her own to Les' open face. The blow drew blood from her thick lips.

"Shut the fuck up! You nasty, perverted bitch! You ought to be ashamed of yourself," Tory voiced. Terry's presence now gave her a sense of pluck she'd never felt before. She felt safe and was ready for some get-back.

"So, what you think we should do, lil sis?" Terry asked in a suggestive tone.

Tory grabbed one of the whips out of the suitcase and smacked Les on the ass so hard it left welts.

"Ahhh! Shit!" Les let out a scream.

Smack! Smack! Smack! Tory struck her again and again and again.

"Shut up, bitch!" Tory hissed.

She looked up at Terry who was quiet and calm during the whole duration of the encounter and said, "I think it's fair enough that I do to her exactly what she tried to do to me!" Then she smacked the shit out of Les again for good measure.

"Ahhh! Tory, please, you ain't gotta do me like—"

Smack! "Bitch, please! Ain't that what I been saying to you for years?" Tory cracked her knuckles. "Shit… you never listened to my cries, so you can save yours!" Tory said as she unstrapped the leather harness from Les and tightened it around her own small waist.

"Tory, I swear, if you stick that—" Les started.

Smack! Tory backhanded her again. "No back talk, remember? Oh, and if you run, it will only make things worse. Terry, do something to keep this bitch quiet, will you?"

Placing the .22 on the nightstand, Terry got a bright idea. Avoiding the colorful assortment of dildos and other sex toys, he retrieved a ball gag from the sexual treasure trove and walked over to Les with it in hand.

Les thrashed around violently on the bed, trying to desperately prolong the inevitable, but Tory was dead set on her intentions and not to be deterred. Les couldn't believe how the tables had turned on her in such a drastic way. She'd always been so dominant, so in control, so strong. Now, she was none of the above. In her forty-plus years of living, Les had only been penetrated by one man. Her own father!

Early on in her childhood as a pre-teen, her father, Lester

McMann, molested and raped her repeatedly. No one believed her when she told them and when he found out she'd run her mouth, it only made the attacks worse and more malicious.

In efforts to keep him away, young Leslie the prissy and pretty girl, became Les the tomboy. Soon Lester's attacks became infrequent and stopped entirely when he died of lung cancer. Les thanked God the day he passed, but she was still broken and very upset she never got to make him pay for the horrible things he'd done to her. The lingering pain and trauma caused Les to act out and become the very monster she was afraid of.

Unlike most victims of such heinous acts, Les' mind absorbed the violence in a different way. Her experiences had an adverse effect on her life, bringing her to the point where she wanted to harm other young girls and act out the sick, twisted, sexual fantasies she'd developed.

"P-please don't... Mmh!" Les' voice trailed off as she struggled with Terry while he attempted to place the ball gag in her mouth.

"Shut up, bitch!" Terry said in a stern voice. A solid right jab caused Les' jaw to go slack and Terry placed the gag on her. With the volume of Les' squeals now lowered, Tory made the last few adjustments on the harness and mounted the bed directly behind Les.

All Les' life, she tried to ruin or distort her beauty in order to seem unattractive to the opposite sex. She cut her hair down and rocked waves deeper than most men. She even worked out to the point where her breasts began to sort of resemble pecs and she even had some faint facial hair. No matter what she did though, there was no way for her to hide the fact that she had that ass! She wasn't holding like her neighbor, Tina. Hell, nobody was! But, she definitely had more than a lil somethin' back there.

Lubrication would not be a courtesy for Les, except for the small amount of spit Tory offered her ass crack. Tory dragged the tip of BIG BLACK down the crevice and was stalled out upon first efforts of forced entry.

Les' dark chocolate cheeks were clamped down tight like vise grips. Terry was truly fucked up in the head. The sight of Les' struggle turned him on. Had Tory been anyone else but his sister, he'd have stripped naked and handled his business.

Seeing Tory be denied her revenge enraged Terry, so he reached over Les, placed a firm grip on her ass and roughly parted her ass cheeks like the Red Sea!

"Bullseye, bitch!" Tory teased as she pushed BIG BLACK as far as she could down Les' canal. A popping sound filled the room as the rubber dilated Les' sphincter to accommodate the unnatural circumference. Tory pumped back and forth vigorously, trying to impale Les deeper with every stroke. Every thrust fueled by pain and hate.

The visual, along with Les' muffled moans and groans of anguish, had Terry fighting the awakening below his belt. He wanted in on the action, but he let Tory have her shine. He had to.

Tory thrusted until she broke a sweat, making her reddish-colored hair stick to her face and neck. When she realized that she drew blood performing her back-door invasion, a trickle of guilt made her stop. Tory felt bad, but not bad enough to relieve Les of the pain. So, she slipped out of the harness and left 'BIG BLACK' hanging halfway in and halfway out of Les' rectum.

"Make sure she don't go anywhere," Tory said to her brother.

He nodded, but they both knew Les was in no shape to go anywhere. Not after all that. She would barely be able to walk, let alone overpower Terry and escape.

Tory got the payback she wanted. Well, half of it anyway. Now, she was about to hit Les where it really hurt. Her pockets! She exited the room and returned a few minutes later, with three large duffle bags. The contents at that time were unknown to Terry, but he had an idea.

"Let's go," Tory said, sounding a bit out of breath.

"What about her?" Terry nodded to Les. "I know you ain't lettin' her off that easy!"

Tory then looked over at Les, whose face was covered in tears and her ass in blood. Pride coursed through her veins. She was content with the pain she was able to inflict on her tormentor. Seeing Les suffer like that was priceless.

"She's good. Fuck her! Let's go," Tory repeated.

"Alright, Sis, whatever you say... Just one more thing," Terry said with a devilish grin. He rounded the huge bed where he stood posted the entire time and climbed up on the bed, standing behind Les.

"Terry what are you—" Tory began.

Tory's questioning stopped as Terry brought his foot back like an NFL kicker. He gathered his strength, then kicked the base of the harness BIG BLACK was attached to, with all his might. The giant dildo broke a barrier within Les that Tory couldn't seem to cross. BIG BLACK's full erect length exploded through Les, making a gut wrenching, crunching sound as it unfortunately ruptured her insides.

Les began to bleed profusely and went into shock, seizing up. Tory's eyes bulged. She'd just witnessed her brother go a step too far!

"Oh, my God! Terry, she's gonna di—"

"Sis, fuck this bitch! She ain't have no sympathy for you," Terry said calmly. He went in his pocket and pulled out a Newport and lit it. Little did he know he was about to run a play right out of his late mother's handbook. Sharon would be proud.

"We can't leave her like this, what if she…if she—"

"She won't! Ha-ha. Don't worry, I got this. Where are her car keys?"

Tory made a mad scramble around the room until she produced them. "Here. Let's go, you're driving."

Then the two siblings gathered the heavy duffles, sparing one last look over at Les. Terry blew out his final breath of smoke, before flicking the cigarette butt on the satin bedsheets that held Les' brutalized body. The burning ember of the Newport took only a few seconds before it ignited a small fire that would soon engulf the entire room, then the entire home, while the unruly flames licked away at Les' body, and simultaneously erased all evidence of the twins' presence in the process.

———

"BABY, I think something's really wrong over there. That girl Tory and some guy that looks kind of like her just ran out of the house. They got in Les' truck with three big duffle bags… Oh, shit! Babe, now the house is on fire!" Tina yelled hysterically. She knew how tight BIG D and Les were and considered going over there to help, but the intense streaks of wicked flames dancing in the darkening sky abruptly made her change her mind.

Never again would she get caught in the mouth of pungent flames. Ever! Not by choice anyway. Fuck that! Had Andre not sacrificed himself, she might not have made it out the blaze Sharon started that day so many years ago.

"Damn, what the fuck she got goin' on over there?" BIG D asked.

"I don't know, babe, but I'll keep you posted."

"Please do. Cause I'ma be out soon and somebody gone have to pay for that too!"

———

IT DIDN'T TAKE VERY MUCH for Angela to get Dr. Carson into the bedroom. A few glasses of perfectly aged wine, a bat of her long eyelashes here and there, followed by a sweet sexually charged comment did the trick.

He'd been anticipating this very moment all day... well, years in all actuality. It felt so surreal that things were actually occurring the way he'd always dreamed they would, right in the privacy of his own home.

———

ANGELA WAS DROP dead gorgeous and Clayton Carson thanked his lucky stars for the night she was all his.

Foolishly underestimating Dr. Carson, Angela assumed this once-in-a-lifetime romp would be a quick and easy one, but Clayton had a few tricks up his sleeve. If everything worked in his favor, there wouldn't be a "wham, bam, thank you, ma'am" tonight. He planned to "love her long time."

Six months prior to this chance encounter, Clayton joined an online dating site for seniors. Unfortunately, he struck out with the women he pursued and even the few who pursued him. Due to his occupation in the medical field, he had unlimited access to full vials of Viagra, Cialis and other erection enhancements that he was more than ready to use. Dr. Carson figured the shortcomings of his anatomy was one of the main reasons his ex-wife left him. So, he experimented with a few pills, serums and pumps to give his little guy a significant boost. Much to his surprise, the Pro-Plus liquid and pill combo did wonders for him and Angela was about to see just how much so.

Angela thought she was just going to pull up and put the pussy on Clayton, but as crazy as that sounded, he was about to put some good dick on her.

The reaction Dr. Carson garnered from Angela once they finally fumbled out of their clothes and she saw his pink snake was just priceless.

Now he wanted to see if she could back up all that hot shit she had been talkin' for years…

Their tryst ended up being way more than Angela initially expected, but it was well worth it if this would ensure BIG D's freedom.

Clayton fucked Angela like he hated her for hours, in every position imaginable. He even made her perform some of his more lewd fantasies. Well through the night, bed squeaks, moans, and skin-to-skin clapping could be heard throughout his corridors.

Angela left Dr. Carson's house in the wee hours of the night, feeling like she just left the casting couch of a porn shoot. Now with the hard part of the deal out of the way, she proceeded to the next step. She'd had to speak with a certain someone at Griffin's Mortuary.

Clayton's word was that in three or four days, BIG D would be prepped and ready to go.

CHAPTER 6
FATE OF TWO

As the day began its transition, swiftly fading into a perilous night, Terry continued to steer his twin toward a new, abuse-free life. He'd just rescued her from Hell, but they were still a long way away from anything remotely considered Heaven.

The two rode in silence down the secluded highway for quite some time before either said a word. Their minds were in a constant float between thoughts of the past and present. The things Tory had just witnessed her brother do, coupled with her own actions, were completely out of the norm. She wouldn't dare admit it openly yet, but Tory actually liked the things they did. It made her feel powerful!

That day, Tory's inner demons had been awakened. Demons she would no longer have the strength to suppress. She was a true murderess in the making...

Taking one glance at Tory, Terry could surely tell they were very much alike. She too was a strong individual who had the unfortunate experience of suffering unhealthy amounts of both mental and physical traumas.

Although Terry was maybe only three or four when some

tragic events resulted in the separation of his twin, he retained faint memories of the bond they shared early in childhood. Short flashbacks of their infantry, terrible two's and the dreaded pee-wee three's took him back to the good ole days.

In a blur, memories passed. Everything from the dirty diapers, backyard playtime on the Fisher Price swing sets, and even their unintentional torment of their older brother Terrance came to mind.

Unconsciously, Terry began to smile. A simple turn of the lips that highlighted the handsome features of his face and amplified his youth. His million-dollar grin could fool anyone who didn't truly know him into thinking he was so sweet, your teeth would rot. But deep beneath the surface of his physical being lurked a very deranged and disturbed character. For one to witness Terry's truth, they had to carefully examine his flash-frozen heart. They had to look beyond the veil of his undeniable charm and charisma and gaze deep into the windows of his tainted soul.

The smile only lasted for a split second but was more than enough time for Tory to notice.

"Why the smile?" she asked, obviously puzzled. This was exactly the convo she needed to draw her mind away from the constant looping images of Les' last breath, and focus on something other than the pungent odor of her tormentor's sizzled flesh still lingering on the fabric of their clothes.

"Well, sis," Terry answered reflectively, "honestly, I'm just happy to have you back in my life. I hate the way things have been for you through our years apart and I want you to know from now on, I will always protect you. I got your back, no matter what!"

Taking in her brother's words, Tory's heart began to swell with nothing but love and compassion for her twin. She was beyond happy to reunite with him. In a way, she now felt as if she owed him her life. There was no one or nothing that could stop her from having his back either.

"Thanks, brother! You just don't know how much I appreciate you for doing what you did and getting me the fuck out of there. You wouldn't believe half of everything I've endured with that woman, especially since Momma…" Tory's sentence trailed off as she realized she was about to reveal the fate of their mother.

It wasn't that she didn't want to tell him, because she did. This was definitely a topic that seriously needed to be discussed. It was just that she planned to deliver this harsh blow with much more grace.

"I don't doubt that you've been through hell, Sis. Shit, we have a lot more in common besides our physical appearance and DNA than you think," Terry admitted to his sister, as he tried to quickly push past certain thoughts and memories that were forever linked to his physical and psychological traumas. In efforts to mask the clear underlying message in his words, Terry abruptly played on Tory's earlier slip-up and asked the golden question. "What happened to Momma?"

Unsure where or how to begin, Tory neglected to answer right away. Instead, she asked a serious question of her own. "What happened to Terrance?"

Hearing Terrance's name still sent surges of both anger and pain through Terry's body. Terrance's death was and would always be a sore spot for him. The secret he carried about his brother's death would always weigh heavy on his heart.

Finally, seizing the opportunity to release some of this weight and gain the knowledge of his mother's life that he longed for, Terry glanced at Tory and said, "You first."

Without so much as a fair warning, Tory opened her mouth and revealed the truth. "Momma is dead. She passed about four years ago and ever since then, I've been stuck alone with Les."

Terry swallowed hard, accepting her words without shedding a single tear, even though he did feel a tinge of pain in his chest. He didn't know his mother Sharon as well as Tory, but he did still have some love for the woman, regardless of his trust and abandonment issues. In a way, strange as it was, he was happy to hear that his mother had gone on to glory. At least she wasn't somewhere strung out or rotting away in a Texas prison cell somewhere, he reasoned.

"What happened? How did she die?" he asked.

"That bitch, Les!" Tory yelled, her voice stocked with raw emotion.

"What! That bitch killed my momma? Are you fuckin' serious?" Terry's blood began to boil. He was ready to bust a smooth ass U-turn, go back to Les' crib and kill the bitch again!

"Well... technically, she didn't kill Ma! But she might as well have, it was all her fault!"

"Huh?" Terry was lost.

"See, I was real young when Mom got with Les. From what Momma told me, back then she was in a real depressive and vulnerable state. She was emotionally scarred and facing many financial difficulties. So, she went to see a psych doctor and she ended up on all kinds of different meds. The pharmacy she used to fill her scripts at just so happened to be Les'." Tory turned to Terry and he nodded to show he was still following, but he kept his hands on the wheel and eyes on the road. "During that time, somehow... some kind of way, Mom and Les hit it off and not very long after that, we ended up moving in with her. As you witnessed today with your own eyes, Les was a predator who preyed on the weak. And she had her way with Momma and eventually me," Tory paused and quickly wiped a rolling tear.

"But Momma was really weak and needed to feel loved by someone. Les, being the master manipulator that she was, used that to her advantage and turned Momma's growing addiction to prescription meds into an invisible leash around her neck. Then she pretty much always got it her way. To spare many more embarrassing details and make a long story shorter, Momma ended up overdosing on a blended cocktail of Percs, Xans, Oxys, Vicodin and all kinds of uppers and downers... I was so torn over Mom's death. I didn't know what to do. But, it seemed to barely bother Les. She was happy she now had access to me without Mom in the way," Tory admitted as she wiped the tears falling in clusters from her chinky eyes.

Sincerely, Terry spoke up, "I wish I could somehow rewind time and change all that's happened, Sis. I really do."

"Yeah, you and me both."

"There's one more thing I have to know," Terry said.

"What is it?" Tory engaged.

"Why did Momma leave me and Terrance... what did we do?" he asked seriously.

With that question, Tory was overcome with more emotion and her tears quickly multiplied.

"Nothing!" she answered. "Momma wanted y'all to know you didn't do anything wrong. When she was sober enough and free from Les' grip, she would tell me stories about both of you," Tory said as she looked down at her half-heart birthmark. "She always told me how much she regretted leaving y'all. It was just that you two reminded her so much of our father and she hated him with a passion. She really wanted to get both of you back, but Les wasn't having it. Every time Momma tried to get herself together and started talking like that, Les would drug her into oblivion. I know this for sure though, despite everything, she did love y'all!"

Hearing this from Tory, Terry silently forgave his mother and even apologized for the time he cursed her name and spoke on her absence hatefully.

"So, Dad—" Terry was beginning to form a question when Tory cut it short.

"Don't know much of him outside the fact that he constantly broke Momma's heart. And to keep it real, I really hate him myself! The way I see it, he's the reason for all this," Tory spoke with her hands. "His actions caused our mother to lose her mind, leave you and Terrence, and fall into Les' trap! Trust me when I say, we have Andre Carter to blame for everything wrong in our lives!"

"Andre," Terry said low. He never knew his father's name. Terrence never spoke of him, and he just couldn't remember the man.

"Don't say the devil's name too many times, he may appear," Tory warned.

Terry nodded and kept steering. "Did Momma ever mention any other family we have, or is it just me and you now?"

This question broke Tory's heart because Terry said me and you, not us. She wasn't stupid, she was sure that meant Terrance was gone. But why? What happened? Her mind raced.

"As far as I know, everyone on Mom's side of the family is dead, except for a cousin out in California, but I don't really remember his name. They weren't close. But she did mention that we have an uncle named Mar and a cousin named Tyreke who live in Odessa. We never met them though. Probably never will. They're related to us on Daddy's side, so fuck 'em really."

A few seconds passed in silence as Terry gathered his thoughts. All the new information he was receiving over-loaded his thoughts. Learning the fate of his mother, Terry didn't feel an ounce of remorse for his hand in Les' death. He was actually proud, feeling as though he saved his sister and properly avenged his mother. He realized what happened to Sharon was what it was and he ultimately accepted that. But accepting what happened to Terrence was something he could never do. Especially, since he was the sole witness to his brother's brutal murder. Just thinking of that horrid night made him uneasy and Tory could instantly feel the change in his vibe.

"It's okay, brother, they both are in a better place now," Tory spoke in a consoling way.

"H-how did you know he was—" Terry choked up.

"I don't know. I guess I could just sort of feel it. I can feel your pain," Tory said, touching her heart. "How did it happen? Please tell me he went peacefully."

Terry's solemn look, silence and tighter clench on the steering wheel answered her question. Tory's heart jolted and her pulse quickened, causing both her anger and sadness to boil.

Finding a way to set aside his feelings for the moment, Terry finally spoke and told Tory everything. Every single detail he could remember from the night of Terrence's murder.

Tory was shocked by her brother's horrific revelation. His words so precise and detailed she could see Terrance's death vividly, as if she were present herself that night at Tha Spot, right behind that dusty sofa with her twin. Tory thought accepting Sharon's overdose was hard, but coming to grips with Terrence's execution was surely a hard pill to swallow and harder pillow to sleep on!

What intensified this whole ordeal and made the truth harder to accept was the person Terry said was Terrance's killer.

Growing up, all girls have a celebrity crush, at least once. For Tory, as she aged into her teen years, she'd been head over heels for one man. He was a hometown hero and just the most perfect human being on earth in her young eyes!

Now with Terry's past knowledge, bile built in her throat as her love for Jax transformed into something deeper than hate. She couldn't believe he took her brother's life!

More silence as Terry watched the blow he delivered settle with Tory. Then all of a sudden, he jerked the wheel left in a twitch of nerves as his mind shifted from the distant past to the present. He realized they were still in Les' truck!

"Fuck! What are we gone do with this car? We can't keep drivin' this shit," he thought out loud... Then the light bulb in his brain ignited. He made a swift exit, and he knew where to go. There was only one man in the city who could help him in this crazy ass predicament and his name was Hot Boi.

CHAPTER 7
SOMETHING AIN'T RIGHT

When Hot Boi learned about the murders of Greedy B. and Dee, he did something he normally wouldn't do. He grieved and prepared to attend their funeral, alongside Jax.

As the weeks began to pass after their burial, something about their deaths continued to nag at him. He had many suspicions as to who may have killed them. Shit, they were both some real street niggas so the possibilities were endless. However, through every scenario and possible suspects, Jax's lil brother Marcus never came to mind. Not once!

Now all of a sudden, he's gunned down by law enforcement and being regarded as the shooter in their murders.

"What the fuck?" was the only thing Hot Boi could voice as he watched the news reporter, Gabrielle Rene', cover her segment on live television. Her tale was shocking and immediately caught his undivided attention as she exposed some truth.

See, Hot Boi wasn't a detective by far, but a real thoroughbred street nigga with many talents and connections. He didn't know everything, but he knew things. He knew in his heart there was absolutely no way a bright kid like Marcus committed such a dark act. He just knew...

Gabrielle Rene' said the weapon the police recovered from Marcus' vehicle was an illegally obtained Heckler & Koch MP5, fitted with a scope and laser, shoulder strap, silencer and extended magazine. After immediate testing, the weapon proved to be the very gun that was used to kill Greedy and D. Lee.

This information was strange to hear because although Lubbock wasn't a small city, it wasn't very huge either. Down in West Texas, especially the 806 area, Hot Boi controlled the lawless realm of the gun trade. There wasn't a piece, big or small, sold in the city that hadn't come directly from his hand or at least originated from his mass collection.

An HK MP5 wasn't the most exotic weapon known to man, but it definitely wasn't a commonly used one either. Not in the Hub City at least.

Before his last shipment came in, Hot Boi was sure no one in the city had one. Just a few weeks prior to all the madness stirring about, his Crip patna Jax came through to say wassup and conduct some car business as usual. During that brief visit, Jax introduced him to his new protégé, T.J.

Taking a liking to T.J. and trying to be cordial and accumulate more business, Hot Boi sold T.J. the only HK MP5 to hit the streets of Lubbock. Coincidentally, D. Lee and Greedy get wet up the same night, by the same kind of weapon! Time passed and this whole situation occurred with Marcus and come to find out, it's all behind the very gun he sold T.J.

"What the fuck?" Hot Boi said again.

Could this be an uncanny coincidence that just looked really wrong? Or did he and Jax critically misjudge the character and intent of this T.J. dude?

The universe seemed to be working in mysterious ways this night because as the many "what the fucks" continued their mad scramble through Hot Boi's jumbled mind, he was appropriately given the opportunity to receive the answers he needed when T.J. himself walked into his garage.

Shit was about to get real, real fuckin' quick!

CHAPTER 8

BIRTH OF A MURDERESS

Being in possession of Les' truck didn't even seem like a factor when they first took it. But now as the adrenaline flowing through their veins decreased, and Terry was able to think rationally again, he realized this was not good. This was a direct link to the crime!

He was certain the fire would ruin any and all physical evidence of their presence, but still it's always better to be safe than sorry.

The only place he knew he could possibly receive help with discarding the vehicle was at 806 Customs.

As he arrived at the building, he pulled around back and was relieved to find the entrance to the garage half-open as he did last time.

"Wait here, Sis, let me go in here and holla at this nigga real quick," said Terry.

"Okay, just hurry please. It's dark out here," Tory said as she took in her surroundings. To her, it looked like she was in some kind of fancy junkyard, with an ominous presence lurking behind foreign cars and the sea of dismantled parts. She could feel it.

Following the trail of darkened oil spills, Terry made his way into the garage. He found Hot Boi leaning against a Bentley with his golden .50 cal Desert Eagle in hand, frozen as if in deep thought. He approached cautiously.

The sight of the huge weapon sent chills down Terry's spine, along with Hot Boi's greeting when their eyes met. It wasn't what he expected.

"Fuck you doin' here?" Hot Boi questioned when Terry materialized in front of him.

"Shit, man, I ain't mean to just pop up on you like this, bro. I just... man, I'ma keep it real. Shit, I need some help and you're the only person I know who could do what I need done," Terry shot straight with the man.

"Hmm, it's T.J., right?"

"Yeah, that's me. Jax's uh... uh... protégé!"

"T.J., what is it you possibly think I could help you wit?" Hot Boi asked, trying to get a feel for how to play this situation.

Having no one else to turn to in this situation, Terry had no choice but to be one hundred with Hot Boi. As he told him his dilemma, Hot Boi nodded as if he understood the gravity of Terry's situation, but the whole time the gun never left his hand.

"Okay, lil T.J., I'll tell you what," Hot Boi spoke nonchalantly. "I'll help you... But I need your help first."

"Shit... whatever it is, just let me know, my nigga!"

"Glad you said that." Hot Boi gripped the pistol tighter in his right hand and raised it eye level with Terry, as he approached and before Terry could comprehend what was about to happen, Hot Boi cocked his arm back and knocked Terry the fuck out with the butt of the Desert Eagle…

From the years Terry spent incarcerated in TYC or the county jail, he'd gotten himself in great shape, after being picked on early on during his time in lock down. Suffering the way he did back then, he had no choice but to learn how to fight. The weak were helpless. With a lot of working out and training daily, he became "Ice Water" from the shoulders and as he grew, his one-hundred-seventy-five-pound muscular frame gave him the natural appearance of a prize fighter. There weren't too many people outside of pro fighters who could stand toe-to-toe with him, and they would even have a hard time. Terry was no pushover by far.

But now, caught completely off guard with his nerves already shot, Terry crumbled like a cookie!

Hot Boi, who stood every bit of six foot one, weighed a hundred ninety pounds and harnessed the brute strength of a lifetime mechanic. He had the upper hand at the moment.

Quickly, while Terry was incapacitated, Hot Boi grabbed him and dragged him over to an automatic car lift, where he restrained his wrists and ankles with thick metal chains. Until he got the answers he was looking for, Terry wasn't going anywhere. Shit, and maybe not even then…

Terry awoke suddenly, after enduring a few embarrassing minutes of unconsciousness. His head throbbed, his vision was blurry, and the restraints on his hands and feet let him know the situation he was currently in was not good!

Fuck! *How did I let this shit happen*? he thought as he struggled with the restraints. Then instantly, Terry lost all care for himself, and one person came to his mind… *Tory*!

———

WHEN TERRY WENT inside the garage, Tory reluctantly stayed behind. She wasn't over the day's uncommon events yet and just wasn't ready to be alone. But she complied with Terry's wishes anyway. He had gained her full and unwavering trust.

Luckily, Terry's horrible parking provided a decent vantage point for her to clearly see his every move, as he spoke with the mechanic. Sighing in relief and comfort, Tory closed her eyes for a moment and began to sing along to her favorite 3BG song before it ended, and the overly enthusiastic radio show host began to speak.

"Look out Hub City! What's happenin', this ya boy DJ Matrixxx, and tonight we got something special for y'all on *104.9 The Beat*! Ohh, yeah! We got another exclusive from Hub City Records! Yeah, you heard right. Another exclusive. This right here is a hot new record from a brand new artist from the label named T.J.! I'm bout to play it for y'all. But, I'm tellin' ya now turn ya' systems up, cause this track is lit! Here we go…"

The song completely captivated Tory, as she listened and hung onto every word from the artist. When the track finally ended, explosions fired through Tory's mind as she came to a shocking realization. The voice that was just pumping vividly through the speakers of Les' truck, was none other than the voice she'd begun to register as Terry's!

She couldn't even grasp the truth! Terry had failed to mention that he was a budding music star.

Suddenly shaking out of her thoughts, Tory opened her eyes only to be horrified by what she saw.

Then, without so much as a second thought, Tory made her exit from the vehicle.

———

DETERMINED TO GET SOME TRUTH, Hot Boi went in the second he saw Terry's eyes open.

"Where that muthafuckin' gun at, nigga?" he demanded to know, his gut burning with suspicion of Terry's involvement in the murders of Greedy, D. Lee and Marcus. "You better tell me right now, nigga, or I'm finna burn you!"

The haze started to clear from Terry's eyes as the fuzz washed from his brain.

Hot Boi wasn't one hundred percent positive about Terry's involvement, but he was going to follow his gut. He knew shooting T.J. right away wouldn't get the answers he craved, but still used the gleaming, golden .50 cal to motivate the man he was now holding hostage for interrogation.

As Hot Boi continued to rattle off question after question with increasing anger and impatience, Terry skillfully avoided the line of questioning.

Soon, Hot Boi realized the quarter-sized barrel of his custom Desert Eagle wasn't doing the trick and he decided to employ a new threat.

The exaggerated buzz of the hydraulic lift Terry was attached to literally scared the shit out of him, as the sound triggered movement and his solid limbs began the act of separating.

Hot Boi watched the worry and dread of imminent death spread over Terry's face from behind the control panel. He stopped the machine just as the discomfort set in and Terry began to wince at the building pain.

"Where that muthafuckin' gun at?" Hot Boi repeated.

Struggling through the pain, Terry said, "My nigga, you trippin'! You on some real live law shit right now. I done told you that's my business. You got paid in full, so what the fuck is the problem?"

"Problem is, nigga, three people I had love for is now in the clouds! And the gun that caused all this shit, is now in an evidence locker somewhere. Crazy part is, I know without a doubt it's the exact same gun I sold you! So, now I'm going to give you one more chance to get your muthafuckin' mind right and explain! If I was you, I'd spit the truth out before you piss me off some more. I'm this close," Hot Boi pinched his fingers together, "from losing all my patience and understanding. Any more bullshit from you, I'ma start squeezin' in this bitch, and that's on Crip!"

Hot Boi was dead serious with his intent as the blue blood coursed through his veins, exciting his rage.

Terry couldn't wrap his mind around this unfathomable situation.

Damn, this shit fucked up... he thought. True enough, he'd been in some bad predicaments before but had yet to face certain death. He damn sure didn't like what was about to happen, but was powerless to stop it. Unconsciously, his mind began to shift towards Jax and how he would miss his chance on vengeance. Then more importantly, he thought, *Oh, shit! Tory...*" then he saw her.

———

WITH SPEED and grace she never knew she possessed, Tory moved urgently through the clutter within the yard surrounding the massive customs garage. She breathed heavily but quietly as her chest rose and fell, and her adrenaline raced rapidly beneath her perspiring skin.

In seconds, Tory was inside the very garage where Terry was now captive and she took refuge behind a parked Bentley with its hood up and one tire missing, held up by a steel jack.

As if her twin could physically feel her presence, Terry's eyes shifted from the cannon in Hot Boi's hands and found a connection with hers, when she snuck a peek from behind the safety of the vehicle.

The look he gave her was one she could only take as him begging her to stay out of it. But that shit just wasn't gonna happen! Tory was about to get her brother out of there or die trying... Fuck that!

Off to her left she spotted a shiny, four-way tire iron, next to the car jack that held up the Bentley. Before she knew it, the iron cross was in her tender palms and she was on the move. Hot Boi was none the wiser.

"Oh, so you really think this shit a game, huh, bitch ass nigga?" Hot Boi antagonized from behind the controls of the car lift-o-matic. "Don't worry, I got somethin' fo' yo' muthaf —" A sudden blow to the back of the head stopped his verbal assault mid-sentence, as the crashing impact of the iron took effect and sent the mechanic toppling over, dissolving into a pile of blood and bone atop the control panel.

Absorbed by the shock of Tory's stunt, both siblings remained quiet until the brief silence was replaced by blaring Klaxons. The loud unknown alarm caused immediate panic. As Hot Boi fell over the main controls, his weight depressed certain buttons all at once that caused the machine to malfunction and slowly start to rise.

The timing couldn't have been bizarre or unfortunate for Terry. His heart jumped with terror as the slack in his binding chains lessened each passing second.

"Turn it off! Turn it off now!" Terry exclaimed, as he tried to resist the slow separation. He was strong, but not strong enough.

Instinctively, Tory pushed Hot Boi's motionless body to

the floor and attempted to stop the machine. So many lights and weird shaped buttons stared back at her, she had no clue what to do.

"Tory, please," Terry shouted. "Hurry, I don't know how much longer I can hold on!"

"I'm trying! I'm trying! It's just so many buttons!" she shouted in worry.

"Shoot it! Shoot it now!"

"What you mean, shoot..." Tory caught her words when she caught a glimpse of the Desert Eagle resting off to the side of the control panel.

"Terry, I don't know how to—"

"Just pull the trigger now!" Terry pushed the words through clenched teeth. "Hurry!"

The large handgun felt like it weighed a ton in her small trembling hands. She placed her index finger on the trigger and closed one eye like she'd seen on TV and movies. She took one measured step back and fired the weapon just as Terry began to bellow a feral scream of pain.

The kickback sent Tory stumbling back a few feet and the explosion of gunpowder rang in her virgin eardrums. She rose slowly and stared at the sparkling control panel... or what was left of it. The Klaxons rang no more.

"Ahh!" Terry groaned. "Sis! Sis! Hurry and come help me down! We got to get out of here!"

Without a response, Tory rushed over to Terry and began unhooking the heavy chains. When she finally got him loose, Terry fell over in exhaustion and excruciating pain.

"My shoulder," Terry whined.

"Sit up so I can see," Tory said, sounding all protective.

Terry grunted and struggled, but managed to sit up straight, though his upper half seemed slouched.

"Looks like your left shoulder is dislocated. But it's nothing I can't fix. Hold on. This may hurt a little," Tory told him as she lifted his throbbing arm, massaged around the protruding blade, then in a few swift maneuvers and a stiff yank, the aching subsided.

The fix was complete before Terry's vocal cords could even formulate a scream.

"Ah, how-how did you do that?" Terry asked in amazement as he tried to rotate the sore limb.

Despite the tense situation, Tory mustered a warm smile. "Ma used to be a good nurse. She taught me a few things when she could." As the last word crossed her luscious lips, a stinging pain inflamed on her jaw and the thundering sound of the slap echoed throughout the garage. Hot Boi's heavy hand collided with her smooth cheek with such power, sending Tory tumbling over in agony and shock. The heavy Desert Eagle soared a few feet out of her reach. Hot Boi never saw it.

Terry was appalled at what was happening, but was still unable to do much in his current condition. He slowly back peddled as Hot Boi approached.

"Bitch, you must have lost yo' muthafuckin' mind hittin' me like that! Now I'm finna kill you and this nigga!" he screamed at Tory while he was walking down on her brother.

Slaps from Les was nothing now, compared to a real man. Tory forced herself through the blur she was in and found her feet.

"Man, hold up, bro... shit ain't even got to be like this!" Terry pleaded as he continued to scoot away from his attacker. With a quick glance toward Tory, he saw her gain her footing and head for the abandoned weapon. He had to buy her some time.

"Bullshit if it don't!" Hot Boi said as he staggered toward

Terry, still holding the bleeding wound on his thick skull. He was one tough dude. Any regular man would have succumbed to the pain, meeting death long ago.

When Hot Boi got within striking distance, he lifted his oily Jordan and repeatedly stomped Terry's ribcage.

"Wait! Wait! I'll talk! Chill!" Terry said through blood-filled coughs.

"Oh, now you wanna talk, huh, bitch!" Hot Boi continued through a flurry of kicks before Tory's words gave him pause.

"Hey! You leave my brother alone!" Tory yelled in her most intimidating tone. She was now standing just a few feet behind Hot Boi with the Desert Eagle trained on his chest, center mass. Her face was swollen, her lips bloody and a migraine was building, but she stood on firm feet ready to fire.

Hot Boi turned now to the more serious threat with the quickness. "Bitch, if you don't put that muthafuckin' gun down, I'ma do something real bad to ya!"

The contorted face he wore said how serious he was. Tory hit him hard as hell with that tire iron and she knew he was fucked up about it. Still, she held her ground with the monster in her hands held high.

"Just leave him alone! Let us go and we will be out of your way, mister," Tory offered.

"You crazy as hell if you think I'ma just let y'all walk outta here. This bitch ass nigga killed my homies!" Hot Boi voiced as he inched closer to Tory with both hands in plain sight.

"Don't move!" Tory warned.

Stubbornly, Hot Boi inched closer and closer.

"Sir! Stop! I'm warning you…"

Boom! Boom! The loud blast burst through the interior of

the garage, as Tory instinctively pulled the trigger, striking Hot Boi mid-lunge. Two bullet holes the size of canned goods marked their entry of his chest.

Falling to his knees, Hot Boi's eyes widened in true astonishment with his last breath. He underestimated Tory's gansta, now it was game over! Just before he fell over, Terry and Tory locked eyes through the gaping holes Tory gifted Hot Boi with.

Terry couldn't believe what had just occurred. Now, both he and his twin sister were murderers. What were the odds of that?

"Brother, are you okay?" Tory asked, rushing over to him.

"I'm fine, just help me up please," Terry said, as Tory slid under his armpit and helped him rise. "Are you okay?"

"It's nothing," Tory said automatically, "we gotta hurry up and get you outta here."

They began to make their way through the garage in a hurried pace when Terry said, "Wait a sec," coming to a halt. "We need two more things before we go."

"What?" Tory sounded worried.

"Just trust me. We gone need it," Terry reassured.

As they doubled back through the garage Terry led his sister to the steel gray wall where Hot Boi kept his secret arsenal hidden away. He uncovered the numeric keypad and typed in the passcode he saw Hot Boi enter last time he was there. The screen read back: Pass Code Invalid!

"What the fuck?" Terry said aloud and tried again and again.

Pass Code Invalid!

Pass Code Invalid!

Tory, witnessing his technical struggle wearing his patience thin, said, "Let me give it a try."

Terry gave her a look that said, "If I can't get it open, then how could you?" But Tory was unmoved as she pushed her brother aside.

Wasting no time, she raised the Golden Desert Eagle and pulled the trigger inches away from the keypad. The numeric device exploded in a blossom of sparks and in seconds, the steel wall opened with a tired hiss.

"Pass Code Valid!" Tory said with a smile in her best impersonated electronic voice. Then she blew smoke from the barrel of the weapon and took a mock bow.

Terry could only stare in amazement. Tory was full of surprises and it seemed she was becoming one with the Desert Eagle, Hot Boi so proudly called THE EQUALIZER.

Already having seen the weaponry before still didn't kill the awe factor for Terry. It was crazy to see such an array of death tools. Tory was equally amazed.

"Holy shit, it's beautiful!" Tory squealed with excitement when her eyes came across the rose-tinted .50 cal Desert Eagle with pearl grips. It was the fraternal twin to the gun in her hand.

Before that day, Tory had never shot, held or owned a gun. She wasn't an advocate of violence, and would rather talk than hurt someone, but she was evolving. The gun seemed to cast an aura or glow that drew to her.

"I got dibs on this one!" Tory claimed.

Somewhere within the garage, Terry found some bags and began loading weapons, ammo, gadgets and what seemed to be tiny explosives into the bags.

"Okay, now help me find where he put the keys," Terry said as he hoisted the heavy bags over his sore shoulders.

In no time they found what they were looking for and took

the keys to a white Lincoln Town Car. Something that would get them safely home and wouldn't stand out too much.

"Now we just need to get those bags from Les' truck and wipe down what we touched just to be safe. I wish we could down wipe down the garage too, but we gotta get the fuck outta here. We been here too long and anyone could have heard the shots," Terry noted.

Terry retrieved the bags rather quickly and wiped down the truck thoroughly. Hitting a button on the Lincoln's key fob, the chirp gave away the car's position among the mass of vehicles. It was easy to spot in the dark of night, being snowflake white and one of the only non-foreign cars parked there.

As they got close to the car, again Tory felt a very ominous presence lurking in the shadows. She stopped abruptly and looked around the yard.

"What is it, Sis?" Terry asked, stopping a few paces ahead of her.

"Something's out here," she said in a low whisper.

"Man, stop playing! We got to go, now!"

"I'm serious." Tory stood motionless.

Then off in the distance, a pair of glowing red eyes seemed to materialize and quickly draw nearer.

Almost instantly, Terry shouted, "Oh, shit!" as the large dark figure leapt from all-fours and came sailing his direction out of the darkness.

The massive rottweiler let out the most demonic bark and was only inches away from piercing his fangs into Terry's unguarded flesh, just before another loud boom rang through the night. The bullet from the rose-tinted Desert Eagle landed flush with the dog's oversized skull turning the bone chilling bark into a whining squeak of agony. Death was almost instantaneous for Zeke.

Terry stood there eyes still closed and arms over his face, while Tory not far away, breathed heavily, holding the smoking gun.

"I told you something was out here."

"You almost shot me!" Terry blurted.

"No, I didn't. But I did just save you from being that thing's dinner."

Terry said nothing. She was right.

"Now, come on, let's get out of here and get you to a bathroom," Tory said with a giggle. "I can smell your shit from here."

Slightly embarrassed, Terry said nothing. He knew it was time to go recalibrate and lick their wounds. Plus, he did need a bathroom like ASAP! Shit was real...

CHAPTER 9

GRIFFIN'S MORTUARY

"Hello, thanks for calling Griffin's Mortuary. First and foremost, I want to say sorry for your recent loss and let you know here at Griffin's, we are here in every way possible to help you lay your loved one to rest peacefully. How may I be of service to you?" Griff spoke in such a way that seemed unrehearsed and sincere.

"Yes, may I please speak with Griff? It's imperative that I speak with him and him only."

"This is he, may I ask whom I'm speaking with?"

"My name is Angela and I'm calling on behalf of a mutual friend."

Griff cleared his throat and continued to speak properly.

"Well, Ms. Angela, might I ask whom is this mutual friend you speak of? As I can recall, all of my real friends are dead or in prison, I'm afraid."

"Well, this friend happens to be in federal prison," Angela spoke curtly.

"No disrespect intended, Ms. Angela, but that only narrows the pool of options slightly."

Angela thought for a second then said, "Right, none taken. Sorry, I'm just so nervous," she admitted.

"No need to be. If this is indeed a friend of mine, I'm willing to help in any way possible."

On the other end of the phone, Angela managed a faint smile, thinking of her man.

"He said you'd say that."

"I'm sorry but who is he exactly?" Griff asked, his curiosity rising rapidly.

"Well, I call him the love of my life. But I believe you remember him as BIG D, Derrick Cook," Angela revealed.

"Big D? Oh shit! Man… how's my nigga doing? Wait, wait, oh no! God, no! Please don't sit up here and tell me—"

"No, no, it's not what you think. But it is very complicated."

"Oh! Okay… umm, what's this about then?" Griff sighed with relief. He hadn't spoken with BIG D in ages, and it would be a shame if he passed before he could at least say thank you! Angela's smooth voice brought him back from his thoughts.

"This is about the body of the teenage boy you received today. That boy was our youngest nephew, Marcus."

"Oh, my God! I'm sorry, I had no idea. Trust me, he is in good hands. All services will be free of charge… Damn, I should have seen the resemblance," Griff said with a self-disappointing shake of his head.

"D also wanted me to tell you that the prison where he is located will be in touch soon. He said it's time for code 'Lazarus.' Do you know what that means, Mr. Griff?" Angela questioned.

"Yes, ma'am, I'm afraid I do. I guess it's about time we reunited."

CHAPTER 10
CODE LAZARUS

BIG D lay awake in the confinement of his cell, patiently awaiting the moment he longed for. He was ashamed that his second chance had to come this way. The consequences he now suffered for his past actions were rather tremendous and seemingly unbearable. In desperate times like this, people of faith would usually pray their way through the tribulation. But nowadays, BIG D felt his prayers went straight to God's voicemail and were purposely unanswered. In his mind, only action could help heal the damage that invaded his and his family's peaceful life on the highest level.

As promised, Angela got the doctor on board with their plan. It was rather simple, yet dangerous and could backfire at any moment if not executed to perfection. But what other choice did BIG D have? Technically, he'd already lost his life to the federal penitentiary, and clinically he did die once, so why not go all out in efforts to avenge an innocent soul?

Materializing from thin air it seemed, a slim, clear syringe containing a thick blue liquid appeared in his monstrous right hand. The exact chemical contents of the medical concoction

was unknown to him. All he knew was this blue juice signi-
fied hope, redemption, vengeance and freedom all liquified in
unison. The power emitting from the syringe was abnormal
and it gave BIG D the push and surge in confidence he needed
to follow things through.

At exactly 4:29 am, BIG D silenced the volume on his
radio that sat on the shelf next to his bunk. He sat up straight
and removed the 5X shirt that covered his tattooed and bullet
riddled torso. Effortlessly, he tore a thin strip of cloth from his
white T-shirt to use as a tourniquet around the girth of
his arm.

He adjusted the pressure on the makeshift band until his
arm throbbed and his veins began to bulge in wild patterns.
Then he pressed the plunger of the syringe slightly to remove
any possible air bubbles, squirting a small portion of the blue
juice freely. Pausing for a second, BIG D took a deep breath
then he carefully administered the shot, filling his veins with
the sacred contents.

Quickly, he flushed the cloth and syringe, discarding the
evidence so vital to his federal prison escape. Within minutes,
a chill began to creep over his thick, battle-worn skin. His
breaths became shorter, vision began to blur and his balance
deteriorated. As he fell down in the middle of his cell with a
signifying thud, everything went dark.

A FEW FEET down the run in cell 59, Mike sat quietly,
patiently awaiting the thud. As soon as the unmistakable
sound registered in his ears he sounded off as planned. All he
had to do was make enough noise to get the guard to come
down the run before count and check BIG D's cell. If he could

do that, BIG D promised to bless him, and no one's word was more solid than his.

"Aye! Aye, C.O.! Look out, C.O.! I think we got a man down! In 60 cell! Man down!" he chanted and kicked on his cell door as loud as possible. "Man fuckin' down! I know you hoes hear me! Get off your lazy asses and do your damn job! We got a nigga dying' back here! Yo! C.O.—"

"Alright, alright, Jackson. I hear ya'. I'm coming, now hold your damn horses," the lazy night shift C.O. said as he waddled down the run from the control panel in the middle of the pod.

"Hey, Jackson, what's all the damn fuss about?" the overweight guard asked, seemingly short of breath from the walk up two flights of steep stairs. "What is it, huh? Chow couldn't have been that bad," the C.O. joked.

"Man, I'm all good over here, boss man," Mike replied. "But I think y'all need to check on my mans over in 60 cell like A-Fuckin'-SAP!"

"Is that right?" the C.O. asked incredulously.

"Yo, I'm dead ass! Somethin' ain't right over there," Mike insisted.

"Now what could possibly be wrong with the King?" the C.O. asked. He was well aware of BIG D's infamy.

"Man, I don't fuckin' know!" Mike shouted, as he slapped his cell door and just about scared the shit out of the worthless C.O.

"Alright, alright... Geez, calm down, would you?" the guard conceded.

Mike, being so damn adamant, caused dread to creep into the guard's conscience as he waddled towards BIG D's cell door only a few feet away. He surely hoped nothing was out of the ordinary. Derrick Cook was one of, if not the most important prisoner on the unit. Should anything happen to that man on his shift, Joe Styles knew he'd be in the unemployment line the following week for sure.

Knock! Knock!

"Mr. Cook, please come to the door for a sec. I need to conduct a wellness check," Styles requested. "Mr. Cook, please come to the door... Now!" he voiced with slight agitation, as he tried to peer over the curtain BIG D had obscuring the direct view into his single-man cell.

Still, no response came, and Styles' worry for his job became more apparent. Following protocol, he reached down to his waistband, unclicked the black walkie-talkie from its holster and spoke into it, "Byers!" He released the button and static crackled over the channel. "Hey, Byers!" he tried once more.

"Yeah, Joe, what is it? I'm tryna finish my damn sandwich over here!" the voice barked over the two-way.

"Yeah, yeah. Hey, do me a favor, would you?"

"Okay..." the radio clicked over again.

"Roll 60."

A few seconds passed before the cell door slowly slid open, revealing BIG D's large, motionless body, laid out in the center of the floor.

"Holy, shit!" Instinctively, Styles rushed in the cell and knelt beside BIG D, checking for a pulse. When one didn't register, he immediately yelled into the walkie, "Byers! Get medical down here! We have an offender down... I-I think he's dead!"

———

"CLEAR THE WAY! C'mon everybody, let's go, move it... make room!" Doctor Carson yelled, as he and his assistant, Marley, exited the crowded elevator with the gurney.

"Someone please make themselves useful and get Miss Anderson on the line," Marley chided the crowd.

"Now!" Doctor Carson added as they pushed through the infirmary doors.

———

AFTER THREE ANNOYING RINGS, Vanessa Anderson awoke with a start when she realized the call was coming in through her work line.

"Someone better be dead," she answered drowsily.

"Um, Ma'am, I'm so sorry to wake you at this hour but that's just the thing, well uh, someone is dead I'm afraid. Doctor Carson is requesting your presence in the infirmary immediately," the C.O. on the phone explained.

"Oh, my ... Are you serious right now?" Miss Anderson asked, as she rose out of her Sleep Number bed, settling her pedicured feet into fluffy slippers. Prior to the call, she was in a deep slumber induced by her favorite Plus One vibrator and this call fucked it all up.

"Ma'am, this is no joking matter, I wouldn't dare – "

"No you're right, I'm sorry. I didn't mean to insinuate such a thing... It's just quite shocking to hear is all. Who is the unfortunate we speak of? Have we lost a fellow employee?"

"No, Ma'am. It's a prisoner," C.O. answered.

"Uh-oh, who is it?" Vanessa questioned as she slid into some clothes.

"Uh, I believe the deceased's name is Derrick Cook."

"Oh, shit! I'm on my way!" Miss Anderson said as she rushed out of her on-site home at the federal facility.

———

APPROXIMATELY TEN MINUTES LATER, Vanessa pushed her way through the infirmary doors with a look of pure focus. She couldn't believe the news she just received. She absolutely had to see this shit for herself. Everyone knew how dangerous BIG D was, how clever and surprisingly how resourceful he could be. To make sure he wasn't cooking up some elaborate hoax, she had to confirm his death with her own two eyes.

The entire ordeal had been staged perfectly by Doctor Carson, down to the last detail. He made sure BIG D pulled this stunt when the unit was short-staffed for the night and the laziest guards were on shift. Plus, he made sure to have his most incompetent assistant there that morning. Marley was simply a pretty face and was totally none the wiser to all the underhanded things occurring right in plain sight.

"Where is he?" Miss Anderson demanded to know, as she reached the medical receptionist's desk up front.

"They're in room 2, Ma'am," the woman replied. She continued to file her nails without even looking up at her superior. She was completely unmoved by the warden's agitation.

As Vanessa entered the dimly lit medical room, Marley was in the far corner seemingly filing paperwork pertaining to the newly deceased. Meanwhile, Doctor Carson was just zipping BIG D's supposed corpse up in a thick black body bag.

"Stop!" she yelled.

Startled, Doctor Carson damn near pissed himself. He was

already so nervous, the sudden outburst had him thinking the jig was up. As ordered though, Doctor Carson stopped dead in his tracks, leaving all but BIG D's face covered.

"What happened to him?" Miss Anderson asked, as she approached the slab holding the massive body with extreme caution. She acted as if his death was extremely contagious.

"What happened to him, I can't say for sure, Ma'am. C.O.D. isn't my area of expertise. But if you truly want my opinion, I would say this man suffered a severe heart attack. Given my extensive knowledge of his lengthy medical records here at this facility, I think that's a fair assumption," Dr. Carson said believingly.

"Is that so?"

Vanessa was still in disbelief of some sort, even as she unzipped the cloak of the body bag engulfing the legend in front of her. BIG D was like a mythical creature with unimaginable capabilities.

The millimeter rise and fall of his enormous, gang-insignia-inked chest was invisible to the untrained eye. With her suspicions running high, Miss Anderson decided there was only one way she could confirm BIG D's death.

"Doctor Carson, where's your stethoscope?" she asked politely. Never once did she take her eyes off BIG D, as if he may disappear if she had.

Utter confusion, then pure fear plastered the doctor's face, as he realized what was about to occur. See, BIG D was not truly dead, but only he knew this at the moment. BIG D was simply in a deep catatonic state of cerebral unconsciousness. If one smart enough was to listen hard enough with a stethoscope, the most faint hint of life could be detected even though he was as still and as cold as the dead come.

Thinking swiftly, Dr. Carson moved over to the drawer

where the medical tool was located, and he positioned himself to obscure Miss Anderson's view of his further deceit. In one fluid motion he retrieved the tool, and simultaneously poked a microscopic hole in the round end of the listening device, rendering it completely useless to its user. Now with a renewed sense of confidence, he passed it to her.

As she placed the plugs in her ears, her heart began to race while BIG D's only softly fluttered about. Timidly, she placed the instrument between his pecs, to the left, just above his heart.

Doctor Carson stood over her right shoulder in a ball of nerves, watching carefully. He was silently debating his exit strategy, if anything with this plan should backfire and blow up in his face. No way he could stick around and risk being implicated in such a scandal. At the same time though, letting the roof cave in on BIG D would surely bring him death. He was ready for neither.

Sweat pooled on his pasty neck and liver-spotted forehead as he watched the woman move the device around vigorously in different areas until finally she was satisfied no sign of life remained.

Confident BIG D would no longer breathe another precious breath, Vanessa leaned down to BIG D's deaf ear and whispered her final words to him with such hatred, it radiated from her pores.

"You sick, sadistic bastard… May God have no mercy on your soul. I hope you suffer for the rest of your days in Hell!" Then with all the strength in her body, she cocked her arm back and slapped the shit out of his still corpse.

"That's for my sister Vivian, motherfucker!" she exclaimed, shocking both Marley and Doctor Carson.

Gathering her composure and wiping the lone tear that

escaped her eye, Vanessa turned to the stunned doctor and said, "Now get this piece of shit out of my damn facility!" before storming out the room.

Both completely flabbergasted, Marley and Doctor Carson, just stared at one another briefly. No one ever knew a personal connection existed between BIG D and the warden. Thanks to Vanessa, BIG D didn't end up at this specific federal facility so close to home by chance. It was no coincidence at all. He had killed her sister Vivian all those years ago. So, with Vanessa being very connected, she did everything possible to ensure he landed under her watchful eye. BIG D was sentenced to life in prison and she wanted to see to it that he surely served every bit of that sentence.

But as most know, BIG D was slick as grease. He had cheated death and now eternal confinement. His life was far from over. He was almost free!

———

AFTER RECEIVING the confirmation call to come and acquire BIG D's remains, Griff showed up to the facility in his mortuary's standard black hearse.

Newport cigarette smoke fanned out of the "Death-Mobile" through the slightly cracked driver's side window, as he pulled through the barbed wire fencing. It'd been well over a decade and a half since he'd smoked anything. But at the moment he truly needed it. He was nervous as hell. It had been an equally long amount of time since he'd done anything illegal, vowing to put that part of his life behind him.

That vow was no longer. Now he was entangled in a crime that could very well land him in the very prison he was relieving his friend from. BIG D's time of need had officially brought him out of retirement.

Much to his surprise, the pick-up went as smooth as you'd see in the movies, thanks to Doctor Carson's careful planning. As quick as Griff came, he went, only this time he was not alone.

CHAPTER 11
MARCUS DIDN'T KILL US

A foggy, gray morning greeted Jax as he awoke from his drunken stupor. The midnight black crow perched comfortably on his chest flew away in shock of the sudden uptick in Jax's movement. "What the fuck!" he said out loud. "Where the fuck am I?"

The chill and gloomy background only created more confusion for Jax, as he attempted to shake the alcoholic haze from his brain. Truly unaware of his location, Jax sat still in the misty-like air while he tried to push the fuzz away and gather his wits. The fog around him soon began to disperse, making the sea of headstones more pronounced and was enough of a clue to give him realization of his position.

"Damn," he said to himself, more so than to Greedy or D. Lee.

His head pounded like a Zaytoven trap beat and his eyes were extremely sensitive to the bright light of the morning sunrise, a clear sign of a lingering hangover. In his current state, his memory was shot and not knowing things always made him uncomfortable. Searching for solace, he began to inhale deeply and rub his throbbing temples.

As if his dearly departed comrades sensed his extreme heartache and distress, the half-empty liquor bottle next to him began to shake, then burst supernaturally. Suddenly a wave of sobriety struck him. His eyes opened wide, as everything came rushing back to the front of his brain. Seeing the empty plot spaces only a few paces from where he sat lit the fuse to his rage. The conversation he shared with D. Lee and Greedy the prior night as he attempted to drink his pain away now rang in his mind with crystal clarity.

"Who killed y'all?" Jax asked repeatedly, only to get the same answer.

"Marcus didn't kill us!" Greedy and D. Lee's spirits spoke simultaneously.

Jax was pleased to hear this. He knew there was no way Marcus could have done such a thing to two people he admired as much as he admired him. Still Jax pressed for answers concerning their demise but they weren't so willing to reveal. The dead could be tricky like that with what could and couldn't be said.

"Our killer will get his in due time... Beware of those around you, Jax! Protect the ones you love. We are here now. Your focus needs to be on Marcus. Don't let that detective get away with what he did, he's dirty, Jax! Marcus was set up. Avenge him!" they demanded. "Be careful, sometimes you just can't dodge karma," they spoke quickly, as if they had said too much and were being forced to fade away.

Jax was both livid and extremely hurt by the death of his friends and little brother. They all had perished for nothing in Jax's eyes. He began to question God on how he could allow such tragedy. For the life of him, he couldn't understand it.

Gaining his composure and finding balance on wobbly legs, Jax had a one-track mind to go get some justice of his own for his brother. He was his brother's keeper, always had been.

Peeling away from the cemetery, he instantly began to formulate a plan to assassinate Detective Sullivan. That would help soothe the pain. He figured the best way to do this and actually get away with it would be to catch the detective coming out of the precinct. Perhaps sniping him from an adjacent rooftop. Only problem with that plan was Jax had a lot of weapons, some as unique as they come, but he didn't have a sniper rifle that could get the job done. For a successful hit, he had to have one. And as luck would have it, he knew just where to get one… Hot Boi!

———

THE DRIVE to 806 Customs didn't take long, coming from the Eastside Cemetery. Hot Boi's shop was on MLK Drive in Parkway, right behind the Lucky Bingo, in the hood. So, it was really a five-minute straight shot to him.

Barely 7:00 am, the shop wouldn't open to the public for another three hours. So, Jax had plenty of time to confer with Hot Boi, the man of many trades. Whipping his Bugatti around like a professional racer, Jax pulled around back where he would always make his entrance.

He hopped out the Nipsey Blue super car and walked toward the half-open garage with a brisk pace. The day's sunlight hadn't fully developed yet, but off in the distance Jax could make out the outline of a very still figure in the dirt. As he drew closer with each stride, it seemed like the figure was some sort of animal covered in drying blood.

"Oh shit! Zeke, what the fu—" Jax spat out before he began to vomit the alcoholic contents of his stomach at the grotesque sight of the slain dog. The beast's head no longer existed, and the neck was mangled from an apparent, large-caliber gunshot wound.The bone and brain matter sprinkled about everywhere.

Jax had seen some bad shit and even done his fair share, but for someone to mutilate a fuckin' dog in such fashion was just sick, and showed clear signs of derangement. Evil or not, Jax didn't think Zeke deserved to go out that way. Donald Trump, George Zimmerman or Detective Sullivan... yeah, but not Zeke! Damn...

Then, Jax's current thoughts shifted from the rotting canine he stood over and to its owner... Hot Boi!

"Fuck!"

He turned on his heels and took off like a crazed Usain Bolt, damn near melting the tread on his Balenciaga Runners. His stomach was in knots and his hopes were high for the well being of his friend. Outside of his newfound connection with T.J., Hot Boi was his only remaining confidant. He simply couldn't stomach the thought of losing him too. That would be too much!

With each step, Jax feared the worst. He knew Zeke was like Hot Boi's best friend and that he'd take on the world before he'd let anything happen to that dog. So, to see Zeke stretched out like that sent chills down his spine.

Breathing heavily, Jax entered the garage in a panic.

"A'yo, Beezy! Beezy, where you at, bro? C'mon, my nigga, say somethin'!" he yelled impatiently as he looked around in every direction for his friend. Jax's mind was in such disarray he couldn't properly survey his surroundings. He'd just passed the jacked-up Bentley, slowly back peddling through the massive shop, screaming as loud as he could before he slipped in what he incorrectly assumed was motor oil.

He fell backwards ungraciously into a dark spill of coagulated blood.

"Man, what the fuck is th..." his words trailed, as he sat up and turned sideways coming in close contact with Hot Boi's dead body.

Devastation rocked Jax to his core upon the gruesome discovery. Hot Boi's torso donned holes the size of Frisbees, and his lifeless eyes stared up at Jax accusingly. The view caused Jax to turn and spew the remaining bile from his guts. The tears that welled and fell from his eyes were automatic and flowed freely from their ducts. He couldn't believe what he was seeing. But whether he wanted to believe it or not, it wasn't going to change the fact that Hot Boi was no longer among the land of the living.

Jax's sadness and confusion only further fueled the anger inside him. His thoughts were everywhere at the moment and he was desperately looking for someone to blame for this shit and everything else that was going wrong. He was seething to give somebody the business.

"Sullivan!" Jax hollered. A weak attempt to appease his anguish and inner thoughts. Deep down, he knew the detective couldn't have been responsible for Hot Boi's death. Truth was, Hot Boi had his hands in so much, anyone could have had motive to do him in. In order to kill the culprit, Jax assumed he'd have to murder half of Texas. Shit, but the way he was feeling over Marcus' death, Greedy and D. Lee's and now Hot Boi's, he was ready to do just that! Fuck it!

Jax couldn't stand to see his mans like that. Just helpless, gone, dead! The images would more than likely be etched into his memory forever.

The thirst for revenge caused Hot Boi's arsenal to pop into his mind and called his name. Now with his mind on murder, Jax made his way to the back of the garage where he could arm himself and be fully prepared for the war he was to initiate on those responsible.

The knots in his stomach tightened when he reached the back wall where the weapons arsenal was located… or where it was supposed to be anyway. The locker was as bare as you are when you come into this cold world. The sight of absolutely nothing but steel gun hangers brought Jax to his knees with an exhausted gasp.

"Oh fuck," he whispered, placing both hands on his head.

Now, shit was real and he knew it. Whoever hit Hot Boi and obtained his armory was ready for anything! Military grade weapons, vests, explosives, ammunition… everything was gone! They had it all. But who had it, was what Jax wanted to know. What in the fuck was going on? And why?

Here Jax was thinking he was going to exact some revenge and raise hell and apparently someone else had the same idea. They got the jump and acted first, why? A lot of shit just wasn't adding up to him at all.

For the first time in his adult life, Jax was scared and the thought of being scared only scared him more! He was witnessing his world cave in from all angles. Tuck was locked up. D. Lee and Greedy dead, Marcus dead, Hot Boi dead, and his son Jr., gone! Everything was so fucked up!

It was now clear to him that a war wasn't coming. No, it had already begun!

Usually Jax was dangerous even without being up against

the wall, but now the pressure was so intense he was losing it and freezing up.

He was shaken, alone and had no clue what was going on or what to do next.

In just weeks he felt he was losing the grip on the city he'd been ruling with an iron fist, for the first time in seven years. Everything was changing so drastically, so rapidly. And as bad as things were at the moment, the worst was yet to come.

PART II

"NIGHTMARES COME TRUE"

CHAPTER 12
BIG D'S RETURN

Griff paced back and forth nervously across the linoleum floor in one of the many rooms of his mortuary. Sweat peppered his bald head, as the overhead lights gleamed from it. He was waiting on BIG D to awake from his faux death. Doctor Carson told him the sedative was only good for a few hours and should be wearing off soon. He moved closer to his old friend and reached to check his pulse and heart rate. Everything still felt the same as it did two minutes ago when he last checked. The wait was getting the best of him. Griff was used to death, given the profession he chose to take after his dad passed, but he didn't know how he'd take it if BIG D didn't wake up. That was his muthafuckin' nigga!

Feening for nicotine, Griff turned to grab his pack and light a square. As he flicked the Bic lighter, he caught movement in his peripheral. Behind him, BIG D rose like he was the fuckin' Undertaker, or on some zombie, *Night of the Living Dead* type of shit! His sudden rise scared the shit out of Griff, causing him to choke on the inhaled smoke. "Damn, my nigga! Why you ain't say something… Just raising up like that, fuck wrong witchu?" Griff said between coughs.

BIG D responded with a deep devilish laugh. "Ha-ha-ha! I been up this whole time!"

"Man, that shit ain't funny, mu'fucka! Is you crazy?" Griff scolded.

"Aw, man… just a lil payback is all," BIG D stated lightly.

"You keep on bullshittin', I'ma be on that damn table in a body bag next. Nigga, you know my nerves bad… talking bout payback. You still on that shit?" Griff asked seriously.

BIG D was silent.

"Man look D, you know how—" he stopped when BIG D raised his hand.

"You good," BIG D stated.

"My nigga, I'm serious. Back then, shit was just so crazy, I couldn't do it no more. Then you know I promised Pop and all that—" Griff explained.

BIG D raised his hand again, signaling him to stop, saying, "I know, my nigga, I know. It's all good. I'm glad you got out when you did. Shit, you see what happened to me. I wish I would've listened to you, and I wouldn't be here right now." He swung his huge legs out of the body bag, and over the table he was on. Taking his first step as a free man in over sixteen years felt like taking his first baby steps all over again. "Where am I anyway?" Big D asked, looking around the bare room.

"Oh, you don't remember your second home?" Griff responded nonchalantly.

"The mortuary?" BIG D asked in disbelief.

Griff nodded in confirmation.

"Damn." BIG D felt the sudden chill of the place come

over him. He'd spent many days and nights here back in his heyday. If he and Griff weren't down in the basement loading caskets of dope, then they were torturing enemies right alongside Les, Lil Vicc and GOAT, before putting their dead bodies in the incinerator used for cremations.

A smirk eased its way onto his dark brown face, as he reflected on the last nigga he stuffed in that muthafucka. Then as quick as the smirk came, it was gone, replaced with the look of grief. He was free, but not under the circumstances he'd always thought would bring him back to his old stomping grounds.

Griff sensed the shift in his demeanor and he too realized how fucked up the situation was. Although he wasn't responsible, he felt so bad.

"I'm sorry, Cuz! My deepest condolences go to you and your family," Griff said sincerely.

"Where is he?" BIG D asked with his head down. He was ashamed. He knew Jax and had the opportunity to spend plenty of time with him when he was a child. He was real close to his oldest nephew since he had no children of his own. But he never got to meet Marcus, Kam or Ke' before Mecia had cut him off back then. Of course, BIG D, being the guardian angel of an uncle he was, he had seen all of them from afar, but never actually met them. Now his first up close and personal meeting with his youngest nephew was going to be so one-sided. To top off his guilt, BIG D felt Marcus was dead because of him. Had he not spazzed out in court back in the day, Marcus would be somewhere playing ball. He felt sick!

"He's up in one of the other viewing rooms. I-I uh," Griff stammered. "I been trying to get him ready for the wake. I only stopped when I had to come get you," he said.

"Take me to him."

As Griff led BIG D up to the chrome-plated casket he'd chosen to house Marcus' body, he knew even though he'd done a great job concealing the damage Marcus endured from the bullets, BIG D was going to flip when he saw him.

Griff and BIG D came up together in Parkway and they got into a lot as kids coming into adulthood. Griff knew BIG D all too well. He knew BIG D was a very emotional person, even though he often hid it with his hard exterior. Family meant everything to him—and to see a child, his own nephew —like that was going to be tough, even for a murderous psycho like D.

"Look D, I want to warn ya before you open this casket, that below the neck it ain't pretty. I did what I could, but man… man, the police dude gave him the whole clip. Cuz, shit was crazy! I swear, I'll break my promise to Big Daddy if I ever see that man!" Griff said seriously. "I mean, I know they said he did some crazy shit, but he's just a fuckin' kid…"

"Believe me when I say that muthafucka gon' get his, know that!" BIG D promised. "I won't rest till I get him in the worst way! You might have to crank the incinerator back up." He paused for a second. "Gimme a minute, Cuz."

As BIG D wished, Griff exited the double doors at the back of the church-looking room filled with pews, he closed the door behind him. Now alone, BIG D walked down the center aisle in the direction of the shining casket. His emotions were in overdrive. Taking a deep breath, he raised the top half of the cover and lost the very breath he'd just taken.

Marcus lay there, lifeless. His facial expression was peaceful, his boyish youth quite apparent. *He resembled Mecia in so many ways*, BIG D thought. He reached out and touched Marcus' stiff cheek and a tear slid down BIG D's full face.

"I'm so sorry, Nephew... If I could—" he choked on his words. "If I could take it all back, I swear, I would. I would have just took my 'L.' Shit... really, if I could go back further, I would have never picked the drugs and guns up. Life would have been so different. I can't change the past though..." BIG D spoke from his cold heart. "But check this, that muthafucka that did this... oh, believe me, his days are numbered! I'ma get him. Just give Unc some time and I'ma make it right. Until then, you watch over all of us. Jax, your momma, your sisters and even me, if you can forgive me... I love you, Neph."

BIG D started to close the casket, but something made him lower the velvety white sheet over Marcus' chest first. The funeral date hadn't been arranged yet, so Marcus' body hadn't been clothed yet. Seeing his nephew's bullet-riddled torso so damaged and caved in, damn near made BIG D's heart stop. In that moment, all sadness left BIG D's mind, replaced by anger and extreme thoughts. He was surely about to act a damn fool! No doubt about it. He closed the casket top and made his exit from the room. His mind was made up, it was time for action. Deadly action.

Griff was out in the hallway when BIG D stepped out with blood-red eyes and a look he hadn't seen in years. He knew where his mind was, but at the same time he didn't, that was the dangerous part. See, he could look and tell BIG D was on some loco shit, but he had no clue just how loco. You'd never know with BIG D until you knew...

"You aight?" Griff asked, as he sucked smoke from another Newport. His habit was back in full swing. He was definitely a-pack-a-day type of guy.

"I'm good. But any muthafucka that get in my way won't be!" BIG D said coldly. "Aye, you still got one of those rooms wit all the clothes for dead people, right?"

Griff looked at his patna with confusion. "Uh, yeah... wassup?"

Well as you can see, I need some gear," BIG D said, looking over his attire. All he had on was his facility-issued white pants, socks and an I.D. bracelet.

"Damn, you right! Shit, I didn't even think about clothes," Griff admitted. "Shit, c'mon."

They entered the wardrobe room and searched forever through the racks to find something to accommodate BIG D's sheer size.

"Shit, you don't keep anything for grown men, do ya?" BIG D joked, squeezing into a tight black suit and dress shoes.

"Everybody don't get this damn big, my nigga," Griff reasoned. Finally, they got that situated and Griff asked, "Okay, what's next?"

"Now, I need a few more favors."

"You name it, you got it," Griff said.

"First, I need to use one of your cars."

"Aight." Griff dug in his pocket and tossed BIG D the keys to the hearse they'd just made his great escape in.

"Cool," BIG D said, catching the keys.

"Now I need to borrow 'BOOMER'."

"BOOMER?" Griff had to make sure he heard right.

"Yeah, nigga. 'BOOMER'... you still got it, don't ya? I know you do!" BIG D snapped.

"You's a crazy muthafucka, you know that, right?" Griff grilled.

BIG D just smirked, his diamond teeth sparkling with the hall's lighting.

"You 'posed to be dead and you tryna go back to the feds! This crazy mu…" Griff was going off as he went to the basement to get what BIG D requested. Somewhat reluctant, he got it anyway.

Shortly, he returned with a long, hard plastic suitcase with a rocket decal of some sort on it and gave it to BIG D.

"Man, be careful with that shit!" Griff warned.

"I don't think that's the point," BIG D quipped sarcastically.

"Yeah… whatever, nigga." Griff took out another square and put it to his lips. Before he lit it, he said, "You need anything else?"

"Yeah. You." BIG D extended his hand.

"You know I'm retired. But, you my nigga. Shit get too hectic, you know I'ma come runnin' if you call!" Griff extended his hand. They locked C's, then embraced in a G-hug.

"Say no more. I 'preciate you doing this solid for me. Stay up, I'll be in touch."

With that said, BIG D grabbed the case and left. He was headed to take care of business.

Using the hearse's old-school car phone, BIG D dialed Angela's number. A few short rings later, she answered.

"Hello?"

"I'm home," BIG D said in his deep voice.

"Oh, my God! Baby, where are you? I'm coming to get you right now!" Angela said, flying out of bed. She was too ready to see him.

"Relax, I have to take care of a few things first. I just wanted to let you know I made it."

"Baby, I love you so much! I can't wait to see you. Do you need anything?"

"No. You've done enough, baby. I'll be by later tonight. Be ready for me," BIG D said before he hung up. He loved Angela dearly, but business came first.

CHAPTER 13
YOU READY?

OMB Peezy's voice carried on in a low rumble from a Beats
Pill, somewhere in the room. His rhetoric of having somethin'
that would make niggas "Lay Down," correlated perfectly
with the scene unfolding in Lil Vicc's living room.

"All that wolfin' like you bout dat shit/ Well, I got somethin' to make ya lay down/ Murda, Murda, Murda, Kill, Kill,
goin' through a nigga mind when I'm loadin' up dem K
rounds/ And we gon' ride through that pussy nigga block one
of these nights and let 'em have it/ Fuck boy, we ain't gon'
play round…"

Tory rapped along word for word, as if she'd penned the
homicidal lyrics herself. Her transition over the last twenty-
four hours was sudden. A classic case of, "Good Girl Gone
Bad." But Tory's case was drastically different than most. In
just hours, she'd turned from victim to victimizer. Once a
novice to imposing violence, now she was feening for it. The
moment she pulled the trigger on Hot Boi, using his own gun,
it transformed her into the murderess she was destined to
become. The power a gun gave her made her complete. So,

the view of the hundred or so that lie in front of her felt heavenly.

Seeing all the artillery brought a sense of joy and excitement she'd never felt. But nothing could replace the rose tinted .50 cal with pearl grips she'd adopted. Just holding the weapon made her pussy moist. Tory couldn't really understand the change she was enduring so quickly, but she just went with the flow. She only knew two things for certain. One, she would never be taken advantage of again! And two, she was riding for her twin brother for whatever, whenever and however!

Tory was really feeling herself. She was enjoying the comfort of a new home with just her brother. The house wasn't nearly as extravagant as Les', but it was nice.

As with most millennials, Tory was obsessed with social media. FaceBook, SnapChat, Instagram, etc. Usually, she wouldn't be one to show out given her natural shyness and distrust of people, but that was her former self. Now, she felt more confident, self-assured and protected. So, she was making videos of herself posing with her .50 cal, making the sexiest gestures she could. Her Instagram live feed was blowing up with comment after comment, as she traded weapons, eyeing the camera sexily and lip syncing a new song by 3BG ft Mulatto, now playing in the background on her Pill.

No doubt about it, Tory was fine as hell. A yella bone chick, shoulder-length red hair, light brown eyes, standing five-eight, weighing about one hundred-fifty pounds, she was curvy in all the right places. Online flashing all her new weapons, she resembled a gangsta version of the singer, Rhianna from the "What's My Name" video with Drake. Niggas was shooting their best shot, sliding in her DMs with a quickness and she was loving every bit of the attention. It was like a new high.

Breaking up his sister's lil video shoot, Terry came into the room after spending an hour putting together the fit he had on. This nigga stepped in, in a pair of black Mike Amiri jeans, black Off-White boxers, black Timbs, a black Gucci skullcap and a bulletproof vest, holding a Tech. No shirt!

"Damn, Soulja Boy! You ready for war or what?" Tory asked, before laughing at her own joke.

"I was about to ask you the same thang, G.I. Jane," Terry said, also laughing.

They both enjoyed each other's humor for a second, knowing they both did look ridiculous, but felt great regardless.

"So, commando, what's the plan?" Tory asked, still cappin'.

"Haha, I see you just full of jokes, huh?" Terry said, as he moved in closer to the weapon cache spread across the room floor. "I got a few ideas, nothing solid yet though. We still got a couple hours to burn," Terry said as he switched the Tech for a new Draco Nano. "How I look?" he asked Tory, while striking a foolish pose holding the Draco Nano.

"Like a damn crook," she replied in laughter.

"Haha, man, you are something else! What am I gonna do with you, sis?" He was rollin'.

"What can you do besides love me?" Tory said in a bubbly tone. Then she swapped her beloved .50 cal for a huge, automatic shotgun. It had a weird ass brand name and sported a 50-round drum. *The gun itself was intimidating, but not as much with Tory holding it*, Terry thought. "How I look?" She copied.

"Like if you pull the trigger on that thing, I won't have a sister anymore. Girl, that thing big as you are," Terry laughed.

"Whatever, nigga, I can handle it!" Tory said confidently. "How about we see if that vest really works." She cocked the shotty with a click-click!

"Whoa. Hell, naw!" Terry said, moving away from the front end of that street sweeper. "My vest work fine. Girl, what's wrong with you?"

"Hahahaha!" Tory slapped her thick thigh. "Bro, I'm just playin'. You should have seen your face. Look like you were bout to shit yo' self again."

"Well, don't be playin' like that!" Terry said firmly. "And stop bringing up old shit!" He was still embarrassed about that incident from the prior night, even though it was funny as hell.

"Aight, shitty, my bad," she relented.

Terry shot her a serious look and she backed off.

"Anyway, where's mine at? I know you don't think you the only one want a vest. I want to look like 50 Cent too," Tory popped off. She couldn't help but joke a lil bit on her brother. That's what sisters were for, right?

"You play too much!" Tory said. "Yours is in the room though, back there next to those bags you brought in from Les' spot. Aye, what's in them anyway?"

"Oh shit, I kinda forgot about that stuff. Go get them and I'll show you," Tory ordered.

Terry returned with the three heavy duffle bags and tossed them on the floor opposite the guns.

"Bet not be full of shoes either or I'ma trip!" he said seriously.

"Nigga, ain't no damn shoes! We gon' be able to buy all

the shoes we want though," Tory said, as she unzipped one of the bags.

"Advil?" Terry asked, puzzled.

"No nigga, them ain't no Advil," Tory said, thumbing through the K-Packs! "These right here are Xanax. These are Percs. These are Molly's or MDMA. These Tabs, Oxys and Vics. And these are XO's and so on," she educated.

"What?" Terry's mind was blown.

"Nigga! Is you slow? These are drugs. Scripts! Uppers, downers, all that shit. Where the hell have you been?" Tory asked, eyeing her brother like a lame.

"In jail!" Terry answered defensively.

"Oh, yeah. You did tell me that, huh? How long did you do again?"

"Shit, too long if you ask me. Been in and out the system since I was twelve." Terry had a slight flashback then said, "But fuck all that. What else you got?"

Tory unzipped the second duffle and they were damn near blinded by the light. Bricks and more bricks of neatly wrapped cocaine appeared. Neither of them had ever really dealt with the drug like that, but it was no mistaking what it was.

"Damn, that bitch was on, huh?" Terry said.

"I guess you can say that. You know where she got it from right?" Tory asked. She knew.

Terry thought about it for a second. It was only one person he could think of that could deliver like this and he barely found out about this side of the man a few weeks ago...

"Jax!" he seethed. "I swear, I'ma push his shit back!" Terry punched his hand.

"We got everything we need to get at him now, that's for sure," Tory said, nodding to the sea of straps. "And I can't wait! Until then though, I guess we can just spend some of this," Tory was saying, as she unzipped the final bag.

"Last time I counted for her, it was three-point-five mil," Tory spoke casually, as if that wasn't shit. She was kind of bougie.

"Three-point-five million what? Dollars?" Terry asked in disbelief.

"No muthafucka, pesos! Duh, dollars!" Tory said, pulling out a stack of hundreds and fanning herself. "Go ahead," Tory egged him on. "Get some. It feels wonderful!"

Yesterday, when Terry went to save his sister, he never thought he was gone hit like this. A while back when he found the forty or so thousand dollars Lil Vicc left behind, he was cool with that. That was the largest amount he'd ever touched. Then when he knocked off Greedy and D. Lee and skated with their bag with a half-million in it, he thought with that amount, he was great. Now, three-point-five mil? Words couldn't describe all the thoughts running through his head. He could tell Tory was used to the money. But he and T.C. grew up on next to nothing, living in the projects with their grandmother. That's why T.C. started hustling and gambling. The latter thing is what got him killed. All for the money…

"Count out fifty thousand for me," Terry said to Tory, as he snapped out of his thought.

"That's it?" Tory asked, as if she counted bills out.

"Yeah, that's it for now. I know what we gone do today," Terry said devilishly. It wasn't so much of what he said, but how he said it that grabbed Tory's undivided attention.

"Okay, what's the plan?" she asked, the interest in her voice and eyes apparent to her brother. "We gon' slide on Jax, right?" The thought of busting her .50 cal again at the first sight of Jax was at the front of her brain.

"Not yet," Terry said flatly.

"Then what?" Tory asked. Her hopes now deflated, she was slightly irritated and started counting again.

"Calm down, sis. Believe me, he gone pay! I'll never let what he did to our brother slide, ut before he dies, I want him to suffer! He has to… that muthafucka took everything from me! So now we gotta take everything from him."

"Okay, now we talkin'!" Tory perked up.

"Yeah, I'ma show that nigga the same mercy he showed our brother." Terry, now feeling Tory's energy, got hyped as well. "See, so far I already took out his best friends and right-hand men, Greedy and D. Lee," he admitted. "Remember seeing that shit on the news a few weeks back?" he questioned.

"Oh shit, that was you?" Tory asked with a look of pure admiration. At first, she was kinda having doubts about her twin. But the more he spoke, they were fading rapidly.

"Damn right! Wish I could do it again, shit, fuck them niggas," Terry capped. He sensed how engrossed Tory was, so he continued. "Them niggas was supposed to be real gangstas, real killas, you know? All that good shit. But it was rather easy to take them down if you ask me," he said, while eyeing an MP5 identical to the one he used for the murder. An evil smirk crossed his face. "Then I got his money hungry ass baby momma to slide off with his kid for a nice lil bag. Haha, he ain't ever gone see lil man again! I know that's gone fuck him up. Especially with everything going on right now."

"I want to be just like you. So strong. So cold. So…so heartless," Tory said seriously.

"If you think that's somethin', check this. On top of that, I just got his lil bro murked. And the best part about it is that a cop did it. A white cop at that! I know he gone get away with it too, no repercussions. Ooh, and the way it happened, I made it look like he killed Greedy and D. Lee's punk asses. Man, I know his family gone be hurtin' like a mutha-fucka!" Soon as Terry said that he felt a twinge of pity for Ke'. He didn't want to hurt her, but everyone else, he was like fuck 'em. Trying to get Ke' off his brain, he then threw another fact out there casually, "Oh, and he was real cool with that mechanic you popped last night. So, when he finds out 'bout that shit, he might fuck around and kill himself before I get to anyway," Terry laughed wickedly, this shit was too funny.

"Well damn, sound like the whole family gone. Shit, so who's next?" Tory questioned.

"This next move might fuck up your lil music playlist, but Kam gotta go."

"Wait…Kam? Like 3BG Kam?" Tory was confused.

Terry moved over towards the weapons cache again and just nodded in confirmation to her question.

"What she got to do with making Jax suffer?"

"That's the nigga's sister," Terry revealed. "You ain't know?"

"No shit!" Tory was shocked and somewhat conflicted but fuck it. "Well, sucks to be her, I guess. I did really love her music though…"

"Yeah, that rude ass bitch gotta go. Like ASAP!"

"Shit, if you ain't fuckin' with the bitch, then I ain't either. I'm with ya all the way. Tell me how you wanna do it." Tory pledged her allegiance.

Terry reached down and picked up a small, see-through plastic container. It held six small gray and white boxes, and a black remote with weird buttons. He waved the container at Tory and asked, "Know how to use these?"

"Hell, nah! Boy, I barely learned how to use a gun yesterday," Tory reminded.

"Right… Well, it's all good. These right here are especially for her. Haha, she been makin' mega hits since she hit the scene, so I think it's only fair she goes out with a banger!"

Together, they laughed at Terry's twisted humor. When the laughs died down, he said to Tory, "Hold on, Sis, I gotta make a call." Then he pulled out his phone and made a call to the only other person alive that hated Jax as much as they did.

Terry knew Bundle deserved a lil get-back at Jax too, and he was about to get it, thanks to him.

————

CLAP! Clap! Clap! Clap!

"Ooh, shit! Yes, nigga! Yessss! Fuck this pussy! Fuck me, daddy," Jada screamed as she rubbed her clit furiously, her orgasm approaching.

Clap! Clap! Clap! Clap!

"Throw it back, bitch! Twerk that ass!" Bundle coached, as he pounded that hoe's back out. He had Jada on all fours, back arched, goin' the fuck off. She was close to the edge of the bed, so he stood on the floor, one leg up on the bed, Captain Morgan style. It was quite an exercise for a fat nigga, but shit, he was puttin' in that work. He'd just sucked his thumb a bit and was about to work it into her winking asshole when his phone rang.

"Damn!" he cursed and slowed his strokes.

"No! No, baby, don't stop!" Jada yelled.

Bundle stopped anyway. Shit, the pussy was good, but money always came first in his book.

"Oh, hell no, nigga. I know you ain't—"

"Shut up, bitch... Hello?" Bundle answered, as he hopped out the pussy.

Not one to slow down on a live fuck session, Jada quit complaining and went to sucking on Bundle's manhood while he talked.

"Aye, wassup, my nigga?" Terry asked.

"Talk to me... wassup up wit it?" Bundle said, trying not to moan in pleasure.

"The *big* payback," Terry said.

"Da' fuck is you talkin' bout? And who... ooh shit, bitch... Man, who is this?" Bundle said, checking the phone number. Jada was doing her best shit, and he could barely see straight. He really couldn't think straight either. He didn't know if he knew the number or not, but the voice did sound familiar.

"My nigga, this Terry from County. I used to be yo celly. Shit, is you ready to do what we always talked about and get at this nigga Jax or what?"

Hearing Jax's name instantly made Bundle's blood boil like only that name could. Quickly, he removed his wood from Jada's mouth reluctantly and started putting on his clothes.

"Nigga, you serious?" Bundle asked, as he was looking around for his Jays, trying to avoid all the shit Jada was talking in the background. He moved the phone away from his mouth, "Bitch, shut the fuck up! I don't wanna hear that bull-shit, I got real shit goin' on!" he said, before coming back to the phone.

Terry still heard everything going on and all he could do was laugh. But he told Bundle he was dead ass serious.

"Where you at?" Bundle asked.

"I'ma text you the addy. Tell me, you still know how to

make shit go BOOM, right? Or was you just makin' all them stories up?"

"Oh no, I was for real! That's my specialty, on Blood!" Bundle assured, as he made his way out of Jada's bedroom, trying to escape her verbal assault and whatever it was she threw at him.

"Damn nigga, that how you really gone do me, jus—" He closed the door on her rant.

"Aye, I just sent the addy. Pull up. This shit goes down tonight!"

"Say no mo'. Shit, I'm on the way," Bundle said and hung up. The only way he was feeling in that moment was, joyous.

Bundle was a real certified street nigga! But he hadn't always been. It was more of a secondary option. A road he had to choose, all because of Jax. For Bundle, Jax had fucked up everything. He hated him with a disturbing passion and rightfully so, he felt. Jax had crushed his big dreams and stolen his right eye! Finally, revenge was gone be so sweet...

———

"WAIT, so this nigga, Bundle is gonna be in on this shit with us?" Tory asked Terry with a hint of jealousy. She was enjoying their bonding and really didn't want to share his attention or let anyone in on the payback she felt was rightfully theirs.

"Yeah. Bundle gone rock wit us on this mission tonight, but that's it. The rest, just me and you," Terry promised.

She still wasn't feelin' it. "Why though?" she asked, almost in a childish tone.

"Well, mostly because he knows how to use these," Terry said, showing Tory the container again. "And because honestly, he deserves a shot to hurt Jax a lil bit too. Not as much as us. But still… Jax really fucked over that man."

"What did he do to him?" Tory asked curiously.

"Shit, I'ma let him tell you… He on his way. If you ain't wit it, then just me and you will go."

———

BIG D WEAVED THROUGH TRAFFIC, going the sixty mile per hour speed limit on Loop 289, heading west.

He was heading out west to Jax's mansion. He hadn't seen it personally of course, being that he was still locked up when Jax had it built from the ground up. Driving through the city felt weird to BIG D. He hadn't been behind the wheel in almost two decades and now suddenly, he was in a hearse on the way to do dirt. Everything he once remembered was now so different, he felt like he was in a foreign country.

Twelve minutes later, he arrived in a very luxurious neighborhood. Almost instantly, he knew which home was his nephew's. It was double the size of the other expensive homes and all the exotic whips out front screamed, "a nigga with too much money lives here!" Plus, there were only three houses, Jax's, Kam's and Stephen's.

Parking amongst the sea of vehicles, the hearse stuck out like a female porn star in a male penitentiary, especially next to Jax's Bugatti.

Stepping out the hearse, BIG D took a second to admire the Bugatti, the Nipsey Blue paint job immediately catching his eye. He reached out to touch the hood and the car was rather warm. Then he knew for sure his nephew was home, and he wasn't making an empty trip.

Jax was inside his home goin' through it. Just a few hours

ago, he found one of his friends shot dead. The day before, his brother was gunned down and his son taken.

The blow from losing his two best friends a few weeks before, that still was fresh. He was beginning to form a wicked sense of paranoia. Ever since he got home a few hours ago, he kept checkin' out the window every few minutes. He was convinced someone was comin' for him and he just wasn't goin' for that shit. He was high as fuck, but on alert! He had his twin Glock 9 "Switches" with the extendos in his hands and was ready to smoke somethin'. The auto pistols would definitely get the job done.

During the brief window of time when Jax wasn't upstairs looking out the window, BIG D managed to slip around to the back of the mansion and enter from a sliding glass door Jax had forgotten to lock. There were so many windows and doors when your mind wasn't one hundred percent, it was easy to overlook one or two. BIG D crept through the home like a cat burglar who'd been casing the place for a while and was there to steal a whole bunch of shit and dip. He was really swift and light on his feet for a big nigga. The home was quiet and showed no signs of his nephew anywhere until...

Brtttt! Brtttt! Jax's Glocks sprung to life automatically, as he pointed in the direction of the intruder.

"Yeah! Muthafucka, I got yo ass now!" Jax yelled in between rounds. He'd cut down a few platinum plaques on the walls and 3BG's most recent diamond one.

Luckily, BIG D's survival instincts still functioned highly. He dove for cover with a tuck and roll as soon as the shots rang out. Not the easiest task for a three-hundred-fifty-pound-man.

"Don't shoot! It's me!" BIG D shouted.

Brtttt! Jax let off a few more slugs in the direction of the voice, tearing up some more expensive shit. He was trippin'!

"Who the fuck is me? And what the fuck you doin' in my goddamn house?"

"Don't shoot! Nephew, it's me, your uncle Derrick! Put the gun down!" BIG D hollered from his cover. He thought he was crazy, but apparently so was his nephew, shootin' shit up in a thirty-million-dollar mansion. He'd definitely developed his "shoot first, ask questions later" mentality. BIG D was actually proud.

"Unc?" Jax said with surprise. "Unc, that's really you?" He still had the pistols pointed in Derrick's direction to be safe.

"I'm comin' out!" BIG D said, as he slowly slid from between the bar, hands up.

As his uncle's unmistakable figure came into view, Jax lowered his weapons.

"Unc! What the fuck you sneaking up on niggas like that for? You almost made me smoke yo ass! What the fuck? How are you even here right now?"

"Thought I'd surprise you. Damn sure didn't think you'd use me for target practice. I'm glad to see you on point though," BIG D spoke nonchalantly, catching his breath.

"Unc, what the fu... how are you here?" Jax asked again, now approaching him.

"I died," BIG D said simply.

"You what?" Jax asked. He was so lost. How could a dead man be present?

"That's how I'm here. The feds thought I died. I didn't, obviously, and now here I am. Now... you just gone stare at me like you seen a ghost, or get over here and show ya' unc some love, huh?"

"Damn, my bad, Unc," Jax said, while closing the distance to hug his uncle. "You scared the fuck out of me!" he said as he embraced him, both pistols still in hand.

"Sorry bout that, Neph. Guess I should have rung the doorbell... or called first, huh?" he realized.

"Ya think?" Jax quipped. "You would realize that... after I damn near killed you and caused thousands of dollars worth of damage to the place," Jax said, nodding to the destroyed plaques and shattered glass riddled with bullet holes.

"You got the money to fix it and I'm a lot harder to kill than you think... You are too. I'll tell you about it one day," BIG D said as he rounded the bar he'd just took cover behind, to pour himself a drink.

"I thought they were here to kill me," Jax admitted, now somewhat relaxed.

"Who is they, Neph?" BIG D asked, as he downed his second scotch.

"I don't know," Jax put his head down. "I'm guessing the same 'they' that's killing my friends and set up my brother."

"Set up your brother?" BIG D yelled. "Who set him up? Where are they?"

"I don't know, Unc, that's what I'm saying. All I know is Marcus was set up. And somebody killed my friends and yesterday, somebody killed my homie, Hot Boi. I found him and couldn't do nothing but leave him there..." Jax started to get emotional. "Unc, I don't know what the fuck is going on... I-I..." Jax was choking up. Overwhelmed with so many emotions, he was breaking down. He couldn't help it.

"It's gone be a'ight, Neph. We gotta stay strong. We gone make it through this shit," BIG D said, as he came around the bar to console Jax. "Get it together," he said, giving Jax a stiff pat on the back. "We got business to take care of. It's time we go pay this muthafucka Detective Sullivan a real good visit!"

"I was gonna get at him earlier," Jax said, wiping his eyes. "That's why I went to see Hot Boi to get a sniper rifle and when I got there..." He wept.

"Don't worry, Nephew. We gone get this muthafucka and we don't need no sniper rifle. It's possible to miss with a sniper rifle. We ain't gone miss with what I got for him," BIG D spoke confidently.

"A'ight, Unc. Gimme a few minutes to get myself right," Jax said as he turned away.

"Aye, Neph, let me see one of those, would you?" BIG D asked, motioning to one of Jax's pistols. Without hesitation, Jax handed one over to D, then headed up to his master bedroom to get dressed.

When he came down, no trace of his earlier emotional state remained. He was stone-faced and cold-hearted. He found BIG D nursing the scotch bottle in the same spot he'd left him.

"A'ight, Unc, I'm ready... let's do this!"

———

MEANWHILE, Bundle pulled up to Terry's house and knocked on the door. Terry was expecting him, so it didn't take him long to answer and greet his old celly.

"Wassup, nigga? C'mon in," Terry gave the invite and a handshake.

"Okay... okay... nice spot, lil nigga. This all you?" Bundle asked, stepping in and looking around.

"Uh, somethin' like that, I guess you can say. This way...

I got someone I want you to meet," Terry said, leading Bundle to the living room.

"Damnnn! Nigga, what kinda shit you got goin' on?" Bundle said when he saw all the weapons on the floor. "This shit is too federal right here! What you sellin' these hoes fa'?" he asked, getting closer to the cache.

"Not for sale," Terry replied, almost too fast.

"Damn, I thought we was better than that, bro... Oooh shit, this hoe clean than a bitch," he complimented on the shotty Tory abandoned for her .50 cal.

"I tell you what. You help me with this, uh mission, I'll let you take any one you want, and I'll pay you fifty thousand," Terry said, cutting straight to business.

"Fifty thousand? To what, kill Jax? Shit, I'll do that for free! All I need is this right here," he said, raising the shotty, "some back up and a live ass plan. It ain't even bout the money, although I could use it. You know bout that situation with my moms and shit," Bundle said.

"Damn, how is she doing, by the way?" Terry asked sincerely. Bundle's mom had an aggressive form of cancer and was going through chemotherapy back when they were in County together. He used to see how fucked up Bundle was 'bout the shit and he really felt for him. Who wouldn't?

"Man, to be honest, she ain't doin' too good. And really, me and my bro Kenny ain't making it no better with all the stress we be causing, doin' the shit we do," Bundle kept it real.

"I hate to hear that, bro. I really do hope she get better though," Terry offered.

"You know, she asked about you about a month ago. I told her I hadn't heard from you. But I guess I can tell her you doin' pretty good now. Enough of all that though. What's the

deal? I walked out on some real good pussy to be here."
Bundle got serious.

"So, I heard, ha-ha-ha," Terry cracked up. "Nah, but let
me let you meet my sis real quick, and we'll get to the point.
Tory, aye, come up here real quick!" Terry called.

"You never told me you have a sister," Bundle said.

"Uh, it's hard to explain, bro."

"I guess." Bundle shook his head. "Sometimes it's hard to
explain Kenny too. That nigga hell!" he laughed.

Tory waltzed into the room like every bit of the stallion
she was and got the reaction she was looking for. Bundle's
mouth dropped and his eyes bucked. She had on her vest,
some all-black form fitting tights, black combat boots, and her
hair pulled up into a tight ponytail that made her facial
features clear. She now held a Draco with the .50 cal holstered
to her stripper hips.

"I think I'm in love!" Bundle proclaimed. He was dead ass
serious too!

Terry smacked him playfully on the head and said,
"Nigga, that's my sister!" Bundle was lost, just staring at Tory
dreamily, he didn't even feel the slap. He only had one good
eye, and he couldn't take it off her.

Quickly, he hopped up and introduced himself, extending
his hand. "I'm Bundle... and you are?"

"Tory... nice to meet you, Bundle." She shook his heavy
hand. She planned to come out and be a straight asshole to the
dude, but she actually liked what she saw and changed her
mind. That, and he didn't seem to be bothered by the Draco at
all, which she liked.

Bundle was a big dude. He was six-three, about two
hundred forty pounds, which was about a hundred pounds
smaller than his old man, but he pretty much resembled the

man in every way. Deep brown skin, piercing confidence that could be seen by everyone, he had a pullout diamond grill, although his father's was permanent and more expensive. Way more expensive. His eye patch on his left eye was probably the biggest difference between him and his dad. For all the physical reasons she could see, Tory sort of liked him and decided she wanted to hear his story.

"So, Bundle, why are you here?" Tory asked, sitting down on the couch with the Draco on her lap. She stroked the weapon like a kitten.

"I'm here to help y'all ride on Jax, right? That's what yo' bro said on the phone," Bundle said, as he looked at Terry.

"That's not what I meant. Sorry, I should have been more specific. See, this whole thing with Jax is real personal to us, and I want to know why you deserve to be in on it. So, I need you to tell me. If I don't like your answer, you're out," Tory stated plainly.

"Y'all serious?" Bundle looked them over. Neither said anything. He looked around the room, saw all the guns again and he knew the answer to his own question. They were serious as hell! "So, what this supposed to be, an audition for murder?" he asked.

"Basically," Tory said as she slid onto the couch close to him and patted the seat next to her. "Let's hear it," she encouraged with an accompanying smile.

Bundle took that as his cue to sit down and run his spiel. Shit, he wanted to get next to Tory's fine ass anyway.

"What you wanna know?" Bundle asked Tory, looking directly into her inquisitive eyes.

"I want to know what Jax did to you. Why you hate him so much?" Tory answered, while staring into his good eye, and the eye patch he wore was appealing to her in a weird way. She smiled again.

"Let me see..." Bundle gathered his thoughts. "I guess in order for you to really understand my hate for this nigga, I gotta tell my whole story, just like I told yo' brother. That cool?"

"We got a few hours still, right, T?" Tory asked her brother, who was fuckin' with the guns again, lost in his thoughts.

"Yeah, till nightfall. We gotta do this when it gets dark," he answered.

"Okay. In that case we got nothing but time. So, shoot," Tory said to Bundle.

"A'ight... shit, y'all smoke? Bundle asked as he pulled out a quarter of some gas and two Original Swisher Sweets.

Tory looked at Terry. Terry looked at Tory and they both shrugged. Tory, being the eldest by six minutes, took it upon herself to say, "First time for everything."

"That's a bet!" Bundle said.

Within two minutes he had the guts busted out the Sweets, the bud broken down and perfectly rolled. He took the red Bic lighter out of his pocket and put some flame on one end of the blunt. Off the first pull, the sweet-skunkish aroma instantly filled the air. He filled his lungs with the precious smoke and began his tale.

"So, it's like this," he exhaled and passed the blunt to Tory, who copied his actions by taking smooth deep pulls. She was doing surprisingly well for a first timer. "Me and that nigga Jax went to school together, right? We played football together and shit. I can't lie, that nigga was cold as fuck! But shit, I was damn good myself," Bundle was saying as Tory exhaled a thick puff of smoke and passed the blunt to Terry.

"Damn, that shit strong," she said, rubbing her chest just over her breast.

"The strongest!" Bundle added.

"I like it!" Tory stated as she watched Terry break in his lungs. "Anyway, so you were saying…"

"Oh yeah, so I was pretty good too. Had like sixteen D1 scholarship offers to play defensive end." Bundle paused amid a flashback of his glory days.

"Ahhk! Ahhk! Ahhk!" Terry cut in with a coughing fit that caught Tory and Bundle off guard.

"Damn, you a'ight?" Bundle asked, reaching for the gas. "That's them 'Gushers', nigga!"

"I'm cool," Terry lied. "Went down the wrong pipe," he said, rubbing his chest.

"Oh, a'ight," Bundle said, reclining further into the couch.

"Rookie!" Tory clowned with a laugh, she was high as hell. "Back to you though."

"So, everything was all good back then. Almost ten years ago now," Bundle was saying, as he touched near his blind eye unconsciously. He was now twenty-seven and the incident that cost him his eye took place when he was just seventeen. "One night after a playoff win, somebody threw a party to celebrate and shit. And I'm sure ya know how wild high school parties can get. That hoe was turnt!" he recalled and passed Tory the dwindling blunt. She grabbed the doobie with expertise, and he continued his tale. "So, I'm in the party doin' me, red cup in hand just enjoying the music and what not, when I get a tap on my shoulder. I turn around and see it's Cori. Now, this white girl was bad, shit, I can't even lie! Before I could see what she wanted, she pulled me close and just kissed me dead in my mouth. Like I said though, the bitch was bad, so I didn't fight it at all," Bundle said admittingly.

Tory exhaled and tried to pass the doobie to Terry, who declined, so she hit it once more and put it out on the coffee table.

Bundle continued, "So as we break our lip lock, she says somethin' like, 'Meet me upstairs in five minutes.' Shit, in my mind, I'm like, bet! I'm thinkin' like, damn this party lit! I'm finna get some pussy and I ain't even have to try. Mind you, I had no clue this white bitch was Jax's baby momma the whole time." He shook his head.

"Aw, shit!" Tory said. She was definitely tuned in. Terry was too, even though he knew the story and exactly how it ended.

"So, here I am, thinkin' I'm all playa and shit, not knowing shit finna go left. I go upstairs and to spare some detail, me and the bitch start fuckin' or whateva. Meanwhile, Jax is downstairs, just gettin' back to the party. Now, I'm thinkin' the bitch just chose up on a real one and threw the pussy at me. Turns out though, she was on some get-back or get-even shit for something she thought Jax did and what not. So, pretty much, she was mad at the nigga and decided to go be a hoe. Even while she was pregnant with the nigga son and shit, which I did not know, she just dry ass drug me into some bullshit." Bundle paused to light the other blunt. He took a few hits and passed it to Tory, then continued.

"I guess when Jax gets back to the party from wherever he went, someone told him what his BM was on. So, the nigga shot upstairs and next thing I know, the door comes flying open. I got my pants around my ankles and shit, so I'm in a real fucked up position. Before I can even understand what's happening… BAM! The nigga catch me with a mean ass hook. I'm struggling to get my pants up so I can defend myself, but this lil muthafucka was so quick wit it and kinda strong... Shit, I hate to admit it, but he got the best of me." Bundle let that linger for a while and hit the blunt a couple more times when Tory passed it back. They were locked in now. Terry was curled up on the floor with an Uzi sleep. "Gushers" got 'em.

Bundle picked up where he left off. "Yeah, the nigga knocked me the fuck out! I guess while I was out, he kicked me or tried to stomp me or somethin', because he fucked my eye up before a few people broke it up. Shit, after that, all I remember was waking up in the hospital with my face the size of a pumpkin and split vision. The doctors told me my eye was so damaged they had to remove it. Man, that shit hurt my soul," Bundle confessed with great emotion.

His story captivated Tory, and she saw why Terry was trying to include him.

"Can I see?" she asked.

Bundle looked at her for a second to gauge her seriousness. Then he leaned forward close enough for her to see.

Tory reached out to him slowly and removed his Dior designer eye patch to see his closed and once battered lid. "How does it feel?" she asked as she rubbed the socket tenderly, before replacing the patch.

"Honestly, I don't feel anything now. It's been so long."

"So, what happened next?"

"Well, after that is when shit went down for real. This why I hate the nigga the most! After I lost my eye, I also lost all my scholarship offers. I guess no one wanted me because I was now considered 'handicapped' and they didn't want the risk. I was never just great academically, so football was my ticket to a better life. Four years of college, then the NFL. That was my plan, and he fucked it all up! Because since then I've always been limited. I can't do this or do that. Can't work here or there. So, my finances have always been limited. And that sucks, because my momma got cancer a lil while back and that chemo shit expensive as hell. Me and my bro Kenny started hustlin' to help with shit. But honestly, that shit only been adding to the trouble. But what other choice I really got? None!

"So, I be out here doing what I gotta do. Shit, I never had my pops around, never knew him. All my moms would say about him is that he was some big-time drug nigga in the city, and she didn't want me in or around that life, so she never told him about me. So, that nigga got a whole kid and don't even know it. It kinda fucks with me 'cause she say he was a big-time kingpin or some shit, so I know he got money! We need money and she refused to fuck wit him, so now I gotta be out here takin' niggas down for crumbs and a chance of goin' to TDC. Shit crazy!" Bundle expressed.

"Damn... that's deep!" Tory remarked.

"Tell me about it," Bundle said, looking to the ceiling. "That's my story though... Fuck Jax!"

"Well, now that I know all that, you definitely in on this mission tonight," Tory approved.

"What's supposed to be the exact plan anyway?" Bundle questioned.

"That's Terry's department right there... Terry! Wake yo' sleepy ass up," Tory yelled, startling him.

"Huhhh?" He hopped up quick with the Uzi at the ready, looking crazy as shit!

Bundle and Tory just busted out laughing. Terry was out of control. Them "Gushers" was a muthafucka!

"I wasn't sleep. I was resting my eyes," he lied. He was clearly knocked out by the weed.

"Yeah... whateva, nigga. What's the plan? Bundle ridin' wit us," Tory informed.

"Oh-oh, now all of a sudden, Bundle ridin' wit us?" Terry mocked, teasing his twin.

"Y'all two somethin' else," Bundle chimed in, laughing at their antics. They were just like him and Kenny.

"For real, brother, wake up. We got to get this all figured out."

"A'ight. You right," Terry said, as he got up, yawned and stretched. "So pretty much, Bundle, like I said... I'ma pay you fifty thousand to do this. You know how to blow shit up, so I want you to rig up some explosives..." He tossed Bundle the container. "...and blow that nigga sister the fuck up."

Bundle caught the container and examined the contents. "Aye, where you get this?"

"Same place we got all this shit," Terry said, waving a hand over the guns.

"You can't just be throwin' shit like this around! You could have killed us all if you accidentally triggered these. You know how much C-4 this is?"

"Hell no, I don't. And don't care as long as it's enough for the job... It's enough for the job, right?"

"More than enough," Bundle assured. "Aye, I hear you on this plan, but what about Jax? That's who I want!"

"Jax is mine. I can't give you that. I told you about T.C. You know I can't give you that. The reason why I'm bringin' you in on this thing with his sister is cause before I kill Jax, I want to break him, and this is part of that process."

Bundle was a fair man, and he understood where Terry was coming from. "I guess I can live with that. But, T, you better let that nigga have it!"

"You think I ain't?" Terry said cockily. "That nigga on borrowed time. My word on that."

"Well, just know if you need me for anything after this, call me. Nigga, my gun smoke too!" Bundle said, as he picked up the shotty.

If Tory didn't like him, she would have protested over Bundle taking the shotty, but he'd grown on her instantly. So, she let it ride.

"A'ight... well, we gone slide by that nigga momma crib tonight. I know Kam gonna be there. So, we gone sneak up and plant the explosives on her whip. Then wait for the right time to blow them muthafuckas!"

"Why not blow the whole house up? Wouldn't that be better?" Tory suggested.

"I'm wit her on that one," Bundle agreed.

"Because that would be too easy. I ain't tryna kill everyone in the house," he said, thinkin' of Ke'. Then he cleared up his statement when he saw Tory and Bundle's disapproving looks. "Yet. I ain't tryna kill everyone in there yet. See, Tory... little did you know the mom is a work in progress already. Remember those pills?"

"You evil bastard! That's what those were for?" she asked, shocked.

"Um-hmm!" Terry nodded. She forgot about the pills.

"You're good! Almost too good," Tory praised.

"I know." Terry dusted his shoulder. "So, let's just do this how I say, and I'll fill you in on the rest as we go, cool?"

"Aye, Captain!" Tory saluted with a laugh that caused Bundle to follow.

"Now, are you ready?" Terry asked them both.

————

As the day's sky-blue shine transitioned into a purple-ish, black star-speckled night, BIG D and his nephew crept slowly down the back streets of Lubbock. They rode in dead silence with their game faces on. One thing and one thing only was on their minds. The exact action they were about to invoke went unsaid, but what was mutually overstood and needed no explanation. Bottom line, Detective Sullivan was about to die! BIG D was about to show Jax a glimpse of his ruthlessness. To ensure the death of one, he'd kill a thousand!

The borrowed funeral vehicle came to a halt about a thousand yards from the Downtown Precinct, discreetly ducked in between two parked vehicles on the brick road. The two men were masked by the cover of darkness, fully prepared to make the whole city light up.

"Show time, Neph," BIG D said, breaking the silence. He pressed a button over his head, close to the rear-view mirror and the partition behind them slowly revealed the back of the hearse. In place of a casket lie the army green case containing what BIG D affectionately called "BOOMER." He reached back and grabbed it and said to Jax, "Are you ready?"

"Hell yeah, I'm ready! Let's get this muthafucka!" Jax was hyped and ready for bloodshed. He checked the clip on his Glock Switch and nodded in approval, but he wasn't going to need the gun. Not on this run.

"That's what I wanted to hear, Neph," BIG D said, wearing a sinister sneer. He was itchin' to get his hands dirty again. Without further ado, he spread the case across their laps long ways and unclenched the clasp.

"Damn!" Jax exclaimed, "Shit, you right, this muthafucka sho' ain't gone miss! Fuck around and clear the whole block with this bitch!"

BIG D agreed with his low-toned, evil signature laugh. The laugh that preceded destruction.

"Where you get this at, Unc?" Jax asked as he admired the one-of-a-kind weapon. Looked like some "Halo" shit.

"You know BIG Unc got connections. Been had this for a while. I would have given this to you back when I gave you the other inheritance, but I didn't need you running around terrorizing the city with this," BIG D said, before he and Jax broke into laughter.

"Haha, I guess you did right! I would have been on some real bad shit," Jax admitted.

"Well, we bout to make it look like the Fourth of July round this bitch. Breaking news, front page of the *Avalanche Journal*, all that shit!"

Jax was all for it. In all honesty, he only wanted Detective Sullivan, but he was feelin' like, *fuck the police*. Then he thought more about the details of things and said, "Unc, wait... what about the cameras and shit? You talkin' bout blowing up a whole damn police precinct and you think we just gone roll up outta here unscathed? You think he still in there?"

"Nephew, you got a lot to learn," BIG D responded with a chuckle, the light from the radio and dash illuminating his million-dollar smile.

"So, you think we finna rock out and they ain't gone do their homework?" Jax was serious.

"Can't do their homework if the dog ate it. I've done my homework and extra credit! I'll never steer you wrong. Follow my lead and we'll be out in five minutes. Watch me work," BIG D said, full of confidence in his ability. "That muthafucka's in there!"

Jax was quite skeptical, but fuck it, he was with his unc every step of the way. Ride or die!

"You see that blue button on your side of the case?" BIG asked.

"Yeah."

"Press it."

Without hesitation, Jax pressed the button to bring the seemingly normal case to life. LED lights lit up in a flash, enabling Jax a better view of the weapon itself, and a few functions of the case. He couldn't explain what he was seeing.

"Whewww!" Jax whistled in astonishment. "What the fuck is this '*I Spy*' ass shit?"

"Well... this," BIG D grabbed the custom three-headed RPG, "this is 'BOOMER'," he explained as he loaded the missiles in place. "And the case itself is an EMP jammer that will block all radio waves, electricity power and pretty much render anything useless for almost an hour. Anything that is already powered on at least," BIG D schooled him and turned off the ignition. "So, with this, the moment we send the charge, there will be no video, no light, no nothing down here for the next sixty minutes. By the time help arrives, the precinct and the muthafuckas inside will be crispy!" he capped with his laugh.

Jax was trying to wrap his mind around this level of savagery. His uncle was a damn fool!

BIG D turned the RPG sideways and Jax damn near jumped through the sunroof!

"Chill, Neph, I haven't even armed this yet," BIG D admonished lightly. "Everything has to be electronically engaged."

Jax slid back down in his seat slowly, still eyeing the three big missiles. "So, what's that?" he asked, obviously still somewhat spooked and rightfully so.

"Well, the missiles are in place, but you have to enable them from here," he said, showing Jax the small monitor with options on it by the trigger guard.

"Oh, shit, I ain't gone lie. You scared the fuck out of me for a second, haha," Jax laughed off his worry. Shit, he wasn't tryna get blown up. Fuck that!

BIG D scrolled through the weapons option list, setting the missiles blasts three seconds apart to maximize the destruction. He was making sure the entire building came down. With a few clicks, everything was set. "Okay, I'm set. Now all you gotta do is pull out the cable antenna, stick it out the window and hold that blue button for five seconds till the charge emits. Everything will go blackout, then I'm gonna get out and set this on the roof, look through the night vision lens and take that muthafucka down! Fuck Sullivan and every other pig in that bitch!" BIG D declared. There was absolutely no turning back now.

Jax carefully studied the case until he found the opening for the retractable antenna. He pulled it out to its full extension, rolled down his window and sat the antenna head on the roof of the hearse, like a cop's emergency lights.

"Okay, now what?" Jax asked and awaited further instructions.

"Now hold that blue button down till all the lights surrounding the case glow green. Once all the power goes off around here, I'm up... I don't want to get out before then and get caught on any surrounding cameras," BIG D stated.

As told, Jax held down the button with minimal force and a growing whir initiated over the next few seconds until the case made a strong vibration, simultaneously flashing a bright green cast of light. All around them the power of buildings, electronics within them and even the streetlights, began to dissipate in a constant roll, until the only power for two square miles was on the glowing case and the RPG's monitor.

"My turn," BIG D laughed out maniacally. In the overly confident way BIG D moved always, he carefully opened the driver door and stepped out, hoisting the weapon of mass destruction on the roof of the car.

Jax turned in his seat to get a better look, there was no way in hell he was gone miss the show.

BIG D held "BOOMER" steady while looking through the night vision target scope. Within seconds, he had the perfect shot and tapped an option on the monitor to confirm the target, locking the sight.

Then, a small, computerized voice spoke. "Target confirmed... Distance, nine hundred eighty-seven yards... three missiles active, on three-second intervals... Fire when ready."

This response garnered a ominous smile from BIG D and without wasting more time, he pulled the trigger.

Shhhhhwuu! The first missile shot off, leaving a tail of thick gray smoke in its wake. Only seconds apart, the second one shot off in the same fashion, followed by the third.

The missiles whistled down the brick road, lighting the pathway with radiant orange-white sparks, one after another like they were in a track race. The first made contact. Boom! Then the second, BOOM! The third seemed to be the strongest, as its blast was elongated and drawn out. BOOOOOOM!

The precinct was up in smoke, crumbling like the Twin Towers of New York on 9/11. The explosions triggered even more explosions from nearby buildings, cars and trucks. The once modest downtown architecture was all up in flames. The fireball of vehicles lining the road mirrored the gateway to the hellish underground. All throughout the blaze, both innocent and guilty suffered unsuspecting issuances of horrible death. Mission accomplished!

———

"SET it off in this muthafucka/ Set it off/ my clique all dogs/ Bitch, don't make us set it off..." Boosie's lyrics had everyone in Bundle's whip turnt! All bobbin' their heads in rhythm, as the bass boomed through the six 12's he held captive in the trunk.

Tory, of all people, was too lit! In the back seat, she dangerously sang the threatening hook into the barrel of her loaded .50 cal Desert Eagle, that she pretended was a mic. She was clearly crazy, but still funny as hell!

"Don't blow yo' brains out in my back seat, girl. I just washed my shit," Bundle joked and shot Tory a shiny white smile through the rear-view mirror.

"Oh, trust me, I won't. I know what I'm doin'. And in case you didn't know, I'm all woman," she said and licked out her tongue at him sexily.

"Uh, I am right here," Terry interjected.

Bundle and Tory just laughed over the music, stealing glances at each other in the mirror again.

They continued to beat down I-20 until they found their exit. Coming off the interstate, blue and red lights accompanied with loud sirens startled all of them, as five cop cars flew by them heading downtown.

"Damn, I wonder what's going on," Bundle said as he decreased his speed to forty miles per hour.

Before anyone in the car could take a guess more cop cars,

ambulances, fire trucks and a news chopper appeared heading the same direction the first motorcade did.

"Shit I don't care what happened. Whatever it is, I hope they keep it long enough so we can do this shit with no problems," Terry spoke up.

"Right!" Tory agreed.

"Right," Bundle said, seeing the logic.

A few minutes later, they turned down Mecia's street under Terry's direction.

"Hold up," Bundle started, "You mean to tell me, this nigga Jax got a net worth of at least a hundred million dollars and his T-Jones still in da' hood? Where they do that at?"

"Shit, I guess in the 806... I ain't gone stunt though, even though her crib is technically in the ghetto, that muthafucka is nice! I'm guessin' they did some remodeling or somethin'," Terry said. "Stop right here. That's it, 'bout three houses down on the left."

"Oooh, her house is cute!" Tory chimed. "Sure you don't want to blow it up too?" she suggested evilly.

"Positive," Terry nixed that idea quickly.

"Aww, you're no fun," she pouted, poking out her bottom lip like a child.

Terry ignored her. Bundle just laughed.

"Matter of fact, bro, whip this bitch around so we can leave the same way we came and not have to drive past the house. That make more sense, right?" Terry said.

"Yeah, it do," Bundle answered as he maneuvered the car around.

"Okay so this what we gone do. It's simple really. We gone get out, go plant the bombs on that bitch's car, sneak back here and just wait."

"That's it?" Tory asked incredulously.

"Yeah, that's it. Shit, what else we supposed to do? Can't blow the car up till she get in," Terry explained.

"And that's why I say we just blow—"

"Tory! We not blowin' that house up! How many times I gotta tell you that?" Terry capped with an attitude. He wasn't killin' Ke', but he couldn't say that.

"Well, excuse me, massa!" Tory responded, folding her arms with a huff, blowing her red bangs away from her eye.

"You ready over there, my nigga?" Terry asked Bundle.

"Shit, let's do it."

They both started to get out, but Tory's voice kept them at bay. "Oh, hell nah! I know damn well y'all don't think yall finna leave me in this damn car," she said, more as a statement than as a question.

"Tory, we ain't got time for all that. Just chill and be still we will be right back," Terry said.

"But—" Tory was saying before Bundle cut in.

"Look, just wait here and when the time comes, I'l let you hit the button," he wagered and surrendered the detonator to her. That deal seemed to calm her nerves enough.

"You see anything funny happening down there, you come bussin'," Terry said, and he and Bundle exited the car before Tory could object further.

The pair struck out down the sidewalk with their dark hoodies on, moving swiftly until they got to Mecia's driveway. They took cover behind a VW Beetle and ducked down.

"You move pretty good for a big nigga," Terry complimented.

"I told ya. What, you thought I was bullshittin'?" Bundle said, breathing lightly.

"Yeah… kinda," Terry said, trying to catch his breath. His adrenaline had his heart beating fast as fuck.

"I can't lie, bro, I thought you might have been bullshittin' too when you used to talk about this shit in the cell, but I be damned if you didn't come through. Shit, look where we at."

"Yeah, ain't no turnin' back now," Terry said, as they looked at their surroundings through the Beetle's windows in a crouched stance.

"You know what you doing with that muthafucka?" Bundle asked, nodding to the Glock. It cast a deadly gleam in the night skies.

You know what you doing with them muthafuckas?" Terry answered, nodding to the more threatening explosive devices Bundle withdrew from the front of his hoodie.

"I can show you better than I can tell you, my nigga. Which car is it?"

"I'd put my money on that pink Range Rover right there that says, 3BGKAM on the plates," Terry spoke with intended sarcasm. Bundle overlooked it.

"Hold me down and watch me work." Bundle didn't wait for a reply, he simply broke into action.

Terry gripped the Glock firmly and cocked it back, readying it for use if necessary. He looked toward the front of the house, the front windows aglow from the light within. He could see slight movement inside the home, but nothing to worry about as long as Bundle moved quickly.

Bundle moved with surprising speed setting the explosives beneath each wheel well, magnets holding the charges in place securely. Each small block lit with a small green light, indicating they were all live and ready to detonate. As Bundle planted the last one and rounded the vehicle back to where Terry waited patiently with the menacing Glock in hand, a car approached from the opposite end of the street.

Terry and Bundle's hearts pumped faster when the hearse

came to a complete stop right in front of Mecia's house. In reaction, Terry raised the pistol and placed a finger over the hair trigger. They crouched lower behind the Beetle and watched the hearse doors swing open to reveal the untimely arrival of another duo.

BIG D STEPPED out the driver's seat into the darkness. He took a deep breath and exhaled smoothly.

"This ain't the hard part, Unc. It's gone be alright. Trust me. She loves you," Jax reassured his Uncle.

"I know, Neph. It's just been so long…" BIG D said as he looked around the neighborhood, his surroundings bringing him back to old memories. "The house looks good. Grandma and Grandpa would have been so proud of what y'all did with the place."

"Yeah, I'm sure they would have. This is Ma's baby, She ain't never going anywhere. C'mon, Unc," Jax said as he rounded the front of the hearse. "Let's go in and check on everyone and start to figure out where we go from here."

As Jax and BIG D made their way to the front door, D suddenly stopped and cast one more look around the neighborhood, his eyes lingering for a while in the general direction where Terry and Bundle hid. Something inside BIG D sensed trouble, he could feel it in his bones. But he figured that with what they'd just done and the many other things he planned to do in the near future, his paranoia was justified. So, he turned and followed Jax inside the house he hadn't stepped foot in over twenty years.

A BIZARRE CASE of curiosity clung to Bundle as he watched BIG D fade into the house. He'd never seen the man before that night, but when he did, he instantly felt like he knew him. And the weird thing was, it felt like BIG D looked right at them, like he knew they were there.

"You think he seen us?" Bundle asked as soon as the front door shut.

"I doubt it. Shit, if he did, I would have been lettin' his fat ass have it by now," Terry said, making gestures with the Glock.

"Man, who was that big nigga with Jax?"

"I'm not positive, but I heard him call that nigga Unc or some shit. Only uncle I know Jax got is BIG D. That muthafucka was in the feds, till now, I guess."

"Wait, wait, wait... BIG D? Like *the* 'BIG D'? The Texas legend, BIG D? Mass murderer BIG D? The—" Bundle was rattling off.

"Yeah, that muthafucka! Why you dick ridin'?" Terry remarked snidely.

Bundle turned to Terry and got serious. "Say Blood, watch that hot shit you talkin'. I fuck wit you, kid. But you got Big Bundle fucked up if you think you finna talk to me like that. That lil thirty-clip ain't gone be enough over this way and that's on me!"

For a cool second, Terry looked shocked at Bundle's charge. Part of him wanted to buck that shit, but not there. There was a time and place for everything. Plus, he was sort of out of line, he realized.

"Damn, my nigga, chill. I'm just fuckin' wit ya'. I'm the ally, not the enemies. All that aggression you displayin' need to be directed toward them muthafuckas in that house! Now let's go and get ready for the show," Terry said with finality and led the way back to Bundle's car.

———————

TORY SAT PATIENTLY in the back seat of the Red Bubble Caprice, hidden behind the tinted windows. The fifteen or so minutes she was alone for what seemed like an eternity. She so badly wanted to press the glowing red button on the detonator. This was her first request the second Bundle and Terry made it back in the car.

"Oooh, can I press it now… please?" she asked with her fingers crossed. She ached for action. Any kind.

"Girl, you crazy as hell!" Bundle said with a laugh. "Patience, young grasshopper. Gotta wait till she get in that muthafucka or we gonna waste good C4."

"Ughh! Story of my life with the waiting," Tory complained. She sighed and looked off to her side, finding something interesting enough to direct her attention elsewhere. "What's all this?" she said as she opened the MCM bag behind Bundle's seat.

Before Bundle could answer or even really knew what Tory was into behind him, the undeniable marijuana stench was consuming the vehicle. The loud pack was supposed to be smell proof, but that shit was bussin' out the vacuum seal!

"That would be the 'Runts'!" Bundle informed. "What you know 'bout that shit, shawty?"

"I know it smell good as hell! And since y'all gonna make me wait… I might as well have some kind of fun, right?" she said with a smile as she watched Terry in the mirror.

All he could do was shake his head.

JAX WALKED down the dimly lit hallway of his mother's home with BIG D on his heels. Before they hit the living room, Jax signaled for D to wait. He wanted to see everyone and feel them out before he made the introduction.

"Ma, I'm home," Jax spoke out, startling the three women in the room.

"Oh, baby! I'm so glad you're okay. We been worried sick," Mecia said as she shot up out of her seat. "Boy, where have you been?" She scolded and squeezed him in a tight hug with strength that contradicted her frame. Jax returned his mother's loving embrace, honestly never wanting to let her go.

"Sorry, Momma," he said, still holding on tight, eyeing Kam and Ke'.

"Boy, where have you been?" Mecia repeated.

Jax wasn't prepared to lie. Not even under the circumstances. When Derrick stepped in and spoke up, he didn't have to.

"He's been with me, Sis," BIG D's voice dominated the room. The three women all gasped with shock.

Mecia's grip on her oldest child slackened. Her heartbeat quickened and her teary eyes widened in astonishment. She could not believe who she was seeing... "How could? Wait a... I thought... Derrick?" she stammered.

TO BE CONTINUED IN...
"HUB CITY MENACE 3"

A Sister's Code
COMING SOON!

SNEAK PREVIEW

PRESS THE BUTTON

"How could? Wait a- I thought… Derrick?" Media stammered. Her eyes were still watering, and the tears wouldn't be held back. They were inevitable.

Live in the flesh, standing before her was her baby brother. The same brother she said she never wanted to see again. The one she blamed and held accountable for the death of their grandparents.

Surprisingly, Mecia rushed over to BIG D and embraced his large form as the flood gates opened behind her pupils. "Oh, Brother… I-I'm sorry…" she tried to speak, holding back gut-wrenching sobs.

"Shh," BIG D soothed his sister, rubbing her back comfortingly as he held her tight to his chest, his chin resting softly on her head of unkempt hair. "It's gone be okay. I'm here now."

"I should have never treated you like that." Mecia squeezed harder. "You never even got to meet him." The waves of emotions were hitting her pretty hard.

"Mec, it's alright. Trust me. I understand your thoughts

and choices. I ain't mad at you. It was all my fault. Everything that happened back then," Derrick was saying as he lifted his chin and began to reminisce a bit. "I was out of control at that point in time, so I get it. It does hurt that I never met Marcus, but he's my nephew and I love him the same," D spoke from the heart.

"My baby's gone…"

"Look at me, Sis," BIG D said to Mecia, lifting her head and wiping her soaked cheeks with a large thumb. "Marcus may not be right in here with us," he said, giving the room a glance. "But he will forever be right here," he clarified with his index finger pointed toward his heart. "We gone figure this shit out, don't worry."

In that instant, all the harbored ill feelings and disdain Mecia once held for her baby brother was gone. Deep down, she knew she couldn't hold that grudge anymore. She had forgiven him for their grandparents' death, and even spoke some to him throughout his incarceration, but seeing him again was just different. Despite their rocky past, she knew that she needed him, especially now. The whole family did.

Mecia squeezed him harder and wept softly, "But they killed my baby." Her heart hurt.

"And I killed them," BIG D stated boldly and without regret as he held her in his arms.

Before Mecia completely understood his words well enough to form a response, Kam's scream interrupted them.

"Oh my God… Look!" She hurried to raise the volume.

———

BREAKING NEWS: "This just in, we have multiple reports on some sort of bombing and or explosion tonight in the downtown Lubbock area. Here's investigative reporter Gabrielle Rene' with more details. Gabrielle…"

"Thanks, Jack. Yes, I'm here at the scene downtown on Main Street, where it is clear there has been a terrible tragedy tonight. Reports began to flood in about an hour ago when the First Precinct of Lubbock was targeted in what is believed to be an intentional terrorist attack. As you can see behind me, there is a solid half mile of raging orange flames the fire department is still fighting to maintain and put out amongst the buildings and scattered vehicles. The nature and reasoning for this attack is still unknown, but there have already been whispers that this could be possible backlash from the recent police shooting of another young African American, or possibly have some connection with the murder of Police Officer Brian Todd, though no direct correlations have been proven at this time.

"I'm sad to say, but further reports at this moment are saying it's believed the City of Lubbock may have just lost almost fifty percent of its law enforcement officers and resources in this devastating blaze that's roaring as I speak. It is a sad day as we all witness the aftermath of this attack occurring in real time. My sources are now saying a few minutes prior to the bombing attack, all the power within the precinct and surrounding buildings was cut, and all channels of communication, both outgoing and incoming were knocked out somehow. This is certainly unlike anything the city has ever seen or experienced before. Exactly how and why this tragic event took place remains unclear, but I can assure you, this investigation will be a top priority and the second we have more of an idea on what's has taken place here, we will be back with an update."

THE URBAN QUESTIONNAIRE

Discussion Questions For The Readers

Questions to Help Form A Full Understanding and Shape Personal Opinions:

1. Picking up right where book one left you, you find yourself coming to terms with what is being set in stone for Marcus. How did Marcus' terrifying death make you feel? Could you see the resemblance in this fictional death and the many police killings of your black males in America today?

2. Do you believe in a "mother's intuition?" If so, explain why. Why doesn't Jax like to be called boss? How'd you take Cori's text?

3. If you were Terry, would you have been upset about missing Jax's initial reaction to Marcus' death? Does the spark between Terry and Ke' blind you to his growing madness? How would you react as Mecia, learning of your child's murder?

4. Under the circumstances, would you separate from your family as Jax did at the morgue to cope? Or would it draw you closer to them? Was Terry wrong for telling Ke' about

Marcus? How would you take the news of a dead family member while imprisoned like BIG D?

5. What did you think of the brutality inflicted on Les when Terry goes to save Tory? Was it not well deserved? Would you consider her former abuse and trauma as an excuse for her actions toward young Tory? If you were to have experienced the life Tory had with Les, how would you exact revenge?

6. Before it was revealed, what had you expected to be said of Terry and Tory's mother, Sharon? Should Terry feel sympathy and have understanding for Sharon's choices? Instead of going to Hot Boi to help their situation, what would you have done?

7. How much love do you have for Hot Boi? Explain how he put two and two together.

8. What did you think of Tory's transformation and how she saved Terry's life?

9. Who does Angela enlist for help in Chapter 9?

10. What time does "Code Lazarus" begin in Chapter 10?

11. Where is Jax in Chapter 11? Explain his supernatural event there.

12. Why does BIG D scare Griff by rising up like the waling dead? What kind of vehicle does Griff give BIG D?

13. In your own words, summarize Terry, Tory's and Bundles' scheme?

Assisted Publishing Packages

BASIC PACKAGE

$699

Editing

Cover Design

Formatting

UPGRADED PACKAGE

$1,000

Typing

Editing

Cover Design

Formatting

ADVANCE PACKAGE

$1,400

Typing

Editing

Cover Design

Formatting

Copyright registration

Proofreading

Upload book to Amazon

LDP SUPREME PACKAGE

$1,700

Typing

Editing

Cover Design

Formatting

Copyright registration

Proofreading

Set up Amazon account

Upload book to Amazon

Advertise on LDP, Amazon and Facebook Page

Submission Guidelines

Submit the first three chapters of your completed manuscript to ldpsubmissions@gmail.com. In the subject line add Your Book's Title. The manuscript must be in a Word Doc file and sent as an attachment. Document should be in Times New Roman, double spaced, and in size 12 font. Also, provide your synopsis and full contact information. If sending multiple submissions, they must each be in a separate email.

Have a story but no way to send it electronically? You can still submit to LDP/Ca$h Presents. Send in the first three chapters, written or typed, of your completed manuscript to:

LDP: Submissions Dept
P.O. Box 944
Stockbridge, GA 30281-9998

DO NOT send original manuscript. Must be a duplicate.
Provide your synopsis and a cover letter containing your full contact information.

Thanks for considering LDP and Ca$h Presents.

NEW RELEASES

BLOODLINE OF A SAVAGE 1&2
THESE VICIOUS STREETS 1&2
RELENTLESS GOON
RELENTLESS GOON 2
BY PRINCE A. TAUHID

THE BUTTERFLY MAFIA 1-3
BY FUMIYA PAYNE

A THUG'S STREET PRINCESS 1&2
BY MEESHA

CITY OF SMOKE 2
BY MOLOTTI

STEPPERS 1,2&3
THE REAL BADDIES OF CHI-RAQ
BY KING RIO

THE LANE 1&2
BY KEN-KEN SPENCE

THUG OF SPADES 1&2
LOVE IN THE TRENCHES 2
CORNER BOYS
BY COREY ROBINSON

TIL DEATH 3
BY ARYANNA

THE BIRTH OF A GANGSTER 4
BY DELMONT PLAYER

PRODUCT OF THE STREETS 1&2
BY DEMOND "MONEY" ANDERSON

NO TIME FOR ERROR
BY KEESE

MONEY HUNGRY DEMONS
BY TRANAY ADAMS

STANDING ON HER BUSINESS 2
BY DG SANTANA

TENDER
BY KHUFU

HUB CITY MENACE
BY JAQUILLE M. WHITE

COUNTDOWN TO A KILLA
CLOCK'S TICKING
BY LO-LIFE

FO'EVA ROLLIN'
BY ASSA RAYMOND BAKER

THUG OF SPADES 3
BY COREY ROBINSON

THE PLUG'S RUTHLESS DAUGHTER 2

BY TONY DANIELS

DYING FOR LIKES
KILLING AIN'T A GAME
BY ARYANNA

GET IT IN SLUGS
BY B STALL

BLOODY MONEY BAGS
VIOLENT LOVE
BY KINGPEN

KILLA CREW
WHAT'S MINE IS YOURS
BY ARYANNA

GUNS DOWN, BOTTOMS UP 2
BY LO-LIFE

MONEY HUNGRY DEMONS 3
BY TRANAY ADAMS

CONFESSIONS OF A DOPEBOY
BY NICHOLAS LOCK

THUG OF SPADES 3
BY COREY ROBINSON

Coming Soon from Lock Down Publications/Ca$h Presents

IF YOU CROSS ME ONCE 6
ANGEL V
By Anthony Fields

IMMA DIE BOUT MINE 5
By Aryanna

A THUGS STREET PRINCESS 3
By Meesha

PRODUCT OF THE STREETS 3
By Demond Money Anderson

CORNER BOYS 2
By Corey Robinson

THE MURDER QUEENS 6&7
By Michael Gallon

CITY OF SMOKE 3
By Molotti

CONFESSIONS OF A DOPE BOY
By Nicholas Lock

THA TAKEOVER
By Keith Chandler

BETRAYAL OF A G 2

By Ray Vinci

CRIME BOSS
By Playa Ray

Available Now

RESTRAINING ORDER 1 & 2
By CA$H & Coffee

LOVE KNOWS NO BOUNDARIES 1-3
By Coffee

RAISED AS A GOON I, II, III & IV
BRED BY THE SLUMS I, II, III
BLAST FOR ME I & II
ROTTEN TO THE CORE I II III
A BRONX TALE I, II, III
DUFFLE BAG CARTEL I II III IV V VI
HEARTLESS GOON I II III IV V
A SAVAGE DOPEBOY I II
DRUG LORDS I II III
CUTTHROAT MAFIA I II
KING OF THE TRENCHES
By Ghost

LAY IT DOWN I & II
LAST OF A DYING BREED I II
BLOOD STAINS OF A SHOTTA I & II III
By Jamaica

LOYAL TO THE GAME I II III

LIFE OF SIN I, II III
By TJ & Jelissa

IF LOVING HIM IS WRONG...I & II
LOVE ME EVEN WHEN IT HURTS I II III
By Jelissa

PUSH IT TO THE LIMIT
By Bre' Hayes

BLOODY COMMAS I & II
SKI MASK CARTEL I, II & III
KING OF NEW YORK I II, III IV V
RISE TO POWER I II III
COKE KINGS I II III IV V
BORN HEARTLESS I II III IV
KING OF THE TRAP I II
By T.J. Edwards

WHEN THE STREETS CLAP BACK I & II III
THE HEART OF A SAVAGE I II III IV
MONEY MAFIA I II
LOYAL TO THE SOIL I II III
By Jibril Williams

A DISTINGUISHED THUG STOLE MY HEART I II & III
LOVE SHOULDN'T HURT I II III IV
RENEGADE BOYS 1-4
PAID IN KARMA 1-3
SAVAGE STORMS 1-3
AN UNFORESEEN LOVE 1-3
BABY, I'M WINTERTIME COLD 1-3

A THUG'S STREET PRINCESS 1&2
By Meesha

A GANGSTER'S CODE 1-3
A GANGSTER'S SYN 1-3
THE SAVAGE LIFE 1-3
CHAINED TO THE STREETS 1-3
BLOOD ON THE MONEY 1-3
A GANGSTA'S PAIN 1-3
BEAUTIFUL LIES AND UGLY TRUTHS
CHURCH IN THESE STREETS
By J-Blunt

CUM FOR ME 1-8
An LDP Erotica Collaboration

BLOOD OF A BOSS 1-5
SHADOWS OF THE GAME
TRAP BASTARD
By Askari

THE STREETS BLEED MURDER 1-3
THE HEART OF A GANGSTA 1-3
By Jerry Jackson

WHEN A GOOD GIRL GOES BAD
By Adrienne

THE COST OF LOYALTY 1-3
By Kweli

BRIDE OF A HUSTLA 1-3

THE FETTI GIRLS 1-3
CORRUPTED BY A GANGSTA 1-4
BLINDED BY HIS LOVE
THE PRICE YOU PAY FOR LOVE 1-3
DOPE GIRL MAGIC 1-3
By Destiny Skai

A KINGPIN'S AMBITION
A KINGPIN'S AMBITION II
I MURDER FOR THE DOUGH
By Ambitious

TRUE SAVAGE 1-7
DOPE BOY MAGIC 1-3
MIDNIGHT CARTEL 1-3
CITY OF KINGZ 1&2
NIGHTMARE ON SILENT AVE
THE PLUG OF LIL MEXICO 1&2
CLASSIC CITY
By Chris Green

A GANGSTER'S REVENGE 1-4
THE BOSS MAN'S DAUGHTERS 1-5
A SAVAGE LOVE 1&2
BAE BELONGS TO ME 1&2
A HUSTLER'S DECEIT 1-3
WHAT BAD BITCHES DO 1-3
SOUL OF A MONSTER 1-3
KILL ZONE
A DOPE BOY'S QUEEN 1-3
TIL DEATH 1-3
IMMA DIE BOUT MINE 1-4

By Aryanna

A DOPEBOY'S PRAYER
By Eddie "Wolf" Lee

THE KING CARTEL 1-3
By Frank Gresham

THESE NIGGAS AIN'T LOYAL 1-3
By Nikki Tee

GANGSTA SHYT 1-3
By CATO

THE ULTIMATE BETRAYAL
By Phoenix

BOSS'N UP 1-3
By Royal Nicole

I LOVE YOU TO DEATH
By Destiny J

I RIDE FOR MY HITTA
I STILL RIDE FOR MY HITTA
By Misty Holt

LOVE & CHASIN' PAPER
By Qay Crockett

TO DIE IN VAIN
SINS OF A HUSTLA

By ASAD

BROOKLYN HUSTLAZ
By Boogsy Morina

BROOKLYN ON LOCK 1 & 2
By Sonovia

GANGSTA CITY
By Teddy Duke

A DRUG KING AND HIS DIAMOND 1-3
A DOPEMAN'S RICHES
HER MAN, MINE'S TOO 1&2
CASH MONEY HO'S
THE WIFEY I USED TO BE 1&2
PRETTY GIRLS DO NASTY THINGS
By Nicole Goosby

LIPSTICK KILLAH 1-3
CRIME OF PASSION 1-3
FRIEND OR FOE 1-3
By Mimi

TRAPHOUSE KING 1-3
KINGPIN KILLAZ 1-3
STREET KINGS 1&2
PAID IN BLOOD 1&2
CARTEL KILLAZ 1-3
DOPE GODS 1&2
By Hood Rich

THE STREETS ARE CALLING
By Duquie Wilson

STEADY MOBBN' 1-3
THE STREETS STAINED MY SOUL 1-3
By Marcellus Allen

WHO SHOT YA 1-3
SON OF A DOPE FIEND 1-4
HEAVEN GOT A GHETTO 1&2
SKI MASK MONEY 1&2
By Renta

GORILLAZ IN THE BAY 1-4
TEARS OF A GANGSTA 1/&2
3X KRAZY 1&2
STRAIGHT BEAST MODE 1&2
By DE'KARI

TRIGGADALE 1-3
MURDA WAS THE CASE 1-3
By Elijah R. Freeman

SLAUGHTER GANG 1-3
RUTHLESS HEART 1-3
By Willie Slaughter

GOD BLESS THE TRAPPERS 1-3
THESE SCANDALOUS STREETS 1-3
FEAR MY GANGSTA 1-5
THESE STREETS DON'T LOVE NOBODY 1-2
BURY ME A G 1-5

A GANGSTA'S EMPIRE 1-4
THE DOPEMAN'S BODYGAURD 1&2
THE REALEST KILLAZ 1-3
THE LAST OF THE OGS 1-3
By Tranay Adams

MARRIED TO A BOSS 1-3
By Destiny Skai & Chris Green

KINGZ OF THE GAME 1-7
CRIME BOSS 1-3
By Playa Ray

FUK SHYT
By Blakk Diamond

DON'T F#CK WITH MY HEART 1&2
By Linnea

ADDICTED TO THE DRAMA 1-3
IN THE ARM OF HIS BOSS
By Jamila

LOYALTY AIN'T PROMISED 1&2
By Keith Williams

YAYO 1-4
A SHOOTER'S AMBITION 1&2
BRED IN THE GAME
By S. Allen

TRAP GOD 1-3

RICH $AVAGE 1-3
MONEY IN THE GRAVE 1-3
CARTEL MONEY
By Martell Troublesome Bolden

FOREVER GANGSTA 1&2
GLOCKS ON SATIN SHEETS 1&2
By Adrian Dulan

TOE TAGZ 1-4
LEVELS TO THIS SHYT 1&2
IT'S JUST ME AND YOU
By Ah'Million

KINGPIN DREAMS 1-3
RAN OFF ON DA PLUG
By Paper Boi Rari

THE STREETS MADE ME 1-3
By Larry D. Wright

CONFESSIONS OF A GANGSTA 1-4
CONFESSIONS OF A JACKBOY 1-3
CONFESSIONS OF A HITMAN
By Nicholas Lock

I'M NOTHING WITHOUT HIS LOVE
SINS OF A THUG
TO THE THUG I LOVED BEFORE
A GANGSTA SAVED XMAS
IN A HUSTLER I TRUST
By Monet Dragun

QUIET MONEY 1-3
THUG LIFE 1-3
EXTENDED CLIP 1&2
A GANGSTA'S PARADISE
By Trai'Quan

CAUGHT UP IN THE LIFE 1-3
THE STREETS NEVER LET GO 1-3
By Robert Baptiste

NEW TO THE GAME 1-3
MONEY, MURDER & MEMORIES 1-3
By Malik D. Rice

CREAM 2-3
THE STREETS WILL TALK
By Yolanda Moore

THE STREETS WILL NEVER CLOSE 1-3
By K'ajji

LIFE OF A SAVAGE 1-4
A GANGSTA'S QUR'AN 1-4
MURDA SEASON 1-3
GANGLAND CARTEL 1-3
CHI'RAQ GANGSTAS 1-4
KILLERS ON ELM STREET 1-3
JACK BOYZ N DA BRONX 1-3
A DOPEBOY'S DREAM 1-3
JACK BOYS VS DOPE BOYS 1-3
COKE GIRLZ
COKE BOYS

SOSA GANG 1&2
BRONX SAVAGES
BODYMORE KINGPINS
BLOOD OF A GOON
By Romell Tukes

CONCRETE KILLA 1-3
VICIOUS LOYALTY 1-3
By Kingpen

THE ULTIMATE SACRIFICE 1-6
KHADIFI
IF YOU CROSS ME ONCE 1-3
ANGEL 1-4
IN THE BLINK OF AN EYE
By Anthony Fields

THE LIFE OF A HOOD STAR
By Ca$h & Rashia Wilson

NIGHTMARES OF A HUSTLA 1-3
BLOOD AND GAMES 1&2
By King Dream

GHOST MOB
By Stilloan Robinson

HARD AND RUTHLESS 1&2
MOB TOWN 251
THE BILLIONAIRE BENTLEYS 1-3
REAL G'S MOVE IN SILENCE
By Von Diesel

MOB TIES 1-7
SOUL OF A HUSTLER, HEART OF A KILLER 1-3
GORILLAZ IN THE TRENCHES
By SayNoMore

BODYMORE MURDERLAND 1-3
THE BIRTH OF A GANGSTER 1-4
By Delmont Player

FOR THE LOVE OF A BOSS 1&2
By C. D. Blue

KILLA KOUNTY 1-5
By Khufu

MOBBED UP 1-4
THE BRICK MAN 1-5
THE COCAINE PRINCESS 1-10
STEPPERS 1-3
SUPER GREMLIN 1-4
By King Rio

MONEY GAME 1&2
By Smoove Dolla

A GANGSTA'S KARMA 1-4
By FLAME

KING OF THE TRENCHES 1-3
By GHOST & TRANAY ADAMS

QUEEN OF THE ZOO 1&2

By Black Migo

GRIMEY WAYS 1-3
BETRAYAL OF A G
By Ray Vinci

XMAS WITH AN ATL SHOOTER
By Ca$h & Destiny Skai

KING KILLA 1&2
By Vincent "Vitto" Holloway

BETRAYAL OF A THUG 1&2
By Fre$h

THE MURDER QUEENS 1-5
By Michael Gallon

FOR THE LOVE OF BLOOD 1-4
By Jamel Mitchell

HOOD CONSIGLIERE 1&2
NO TIME FOR ERROR
By Keese

PROTÉGÉ OF A LEGEND 1&2
LOVE IN THE TRENCHES 1&2
By Corey Robinson

THE PLUG'S RUTHLESS DAUGHTER
By Tony Daniels

BORN IN THE GRAVE 1-3
CRIME PAYS
By Self Made Tay

MOAN IN MY MOUTH
By XTASY

TORN BETWEEN A GANGSTER AND A GENTLEMAN
By J-BLUNT & Miss Kim

LOYALTY IS EVERYTHING 1-3
CITY OF SMOKE 1&2
By Molotti

HERE TODAY GONE TOMORROW 1&2
By Fly Rock

WOMEN LIE MEN LIE 1-4
FIFTY SHADES OF SNOW 1-3
STACK BEFORE YOU SPLURGE
GIRLS FALL LIKE DOMINOES
NAÏVE TO THE STREETS
By ROY MILLIGAN

PILLOW PRINCESS
By S. Hawkins

THE BUTTERFLY MAFIA 1-3
SALUTE MY SAVAGERY 1&2
By Fumiya Payne

THE LANE 1&2

By Ken-Ken Spence

THE PUSSY TRAP 1-5
By Nene Capri

DIRTY DNA
By Blaque

SANCTIFIED AND HORNY
by XTASY

BOOKS BY LDP'S CEO, CA$H

TRUST IN NO MAN

TRUST IN NO MAN 2

TRUST IN NO MAN 3

BONDED BY BLOOD

SHORTY GOT A THUG

THUGS CRY

THUGS CRY 2

THUGS CRY 3

TRUST NO BITCH

TRUST NO BITCH 2

TRUST NO BITCH 3

TIL MY CASKET DROPS

RESTRAINING ORDER

RESTRAINING ORDER 2

IN LOVE WITH A CONVICT

LIFE OF A HOOD STAR

XMAS WITH AN ATL SHOOTER

www.ingramcontent.com/pod-product-compliance
Lightning Source LLC
Chambersburg PA
CBHW071208260626
47162CB00004B/1219